STONE OF VENGEANCE

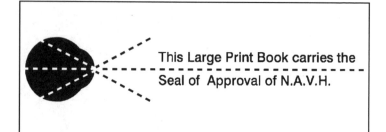

This Large Print Book carries the
Seal of Approval of N.A.V.H.

STONE OF VENGEANCE

109093 — March 2009

VICKIE BRITTON & LORETTA JACKSON

THORNDIKE PRESS
A part of Gale, Cengage Learning

GALE
CENGAGE Learning

Detroit • New York • San Francisco • New Haven, Conn • Waterville, Maine • London

LIBRARY OF CONGRESS CATALOGING-IN-PUBLICATION DATA

Britton, Vickie.
    Stone of vengeance / by Vickie Britton & Loretta Jackson.
        p. cm. — (Thorndike Press large print clean reads)
        ISBN-13: 978-1-4104-1334-5 (alk. paper)
        ISBN-10: 1-4104-1334-9 (alk. paper)
        1. Murder—Investigation—Fiction. 2. Wyoming—Fiction. 3.
    Large type books. I. Jackson, Loretta. II. Title.
    PS3552.R52S76 2009
    813'.54—dc22   2008045208

Published in 2009 by arrangement with Robert Hale Limited.

Printed in the United States of America

3 5944 00109 0933

STONE OF VENGEANCE

Chapter 1

Charles Kingsley, one of Rock Creek, Wyoming's most prominent citizens, lay flat on his back, eyes closed, mass of greying hair spilling back from his pale, fleshy face. He looked so peaceful he could have been asleep — if not for the bullet holes in his chest.

Acting sheriff Kate Jepp's heart plummeted as she knelt beside him. She had just taken over yesterday, and now it had fallen to her to solve the biggest crime in Belle County history. What else could go wrong?

Sheriff Ben Addison, faced with a long stay in the hospital, had overlooked his senior deputies and appointed her as his replacement and this had caused untold havoc in the department. From the moment he had hired her two months ago, she had according to them three strikes against her: she was young and inexperienced, fresh out of the Michigan Police Academy and worst of all, she was not a local. Since Ben had left her in charge, she had tried unsuccessfully to humour the other two deputies, to ignore the undercurrents of resentment toward her that continually surfaced.

Lem Blye, a thin balding man nearing retirement age, carefully ignored her and addressed Jeff Ryman. 'Looks like a simple case of break and enter,' he said. 'During the night Kingsley caught some intruder in his study. They fought and the robber killed him.'

Not satisfied with that conclusion, Kate continued to examine the body. What she found startled her: a stone had been deliberately placed beneath the victim's head. About the size of an open palm, it looked flat, grey and ominous.

Not able to overcome her surprise, Kate, deep in thought, rose and wandered toward the shattered glass of the door that opened onto a wide, columned porch. Kingsley's colonial-style mansion lay in the centre of vast stretches of rolling land. Kate skimmed the deep draws filled with trees and patches of high grass, brown and gold with the approach of autumn. Her attention locked on a ridge of granite rising from the pasture close to the house.

A clump of granite, just like the hundreds

in the field outside. But why would the killer go out of his way to place a stone under Kingsley's head?

Behind her Jeff, just making the discovery, called, 'What do you make of this, Prep?'

Kate ignored the jibe. Lem Blye had given her little support in the sheriff's absence, but not much guff, either. Not so with the younger deputy Jeff, who sorely resented the advancement he had naturally assumed would be his. Ever since her promotion over him, Jeff had considered it the height of cleverness to change her last name from Jepp to Prep.

Kate turned from the doorway, wishing she did not have to see Kingsley's face again, almost peaceful in death.

Jeff moved the dead man's head slightly to the right. 'A rock,' he said. 'Placed like a pillow.'

'That's the stone the thief used to gain entry,' Lem observed. 'He broke the glass, reached in and unlocked the door, then carried it with him into the house.'

'But that doesn't explain,' Kate responded, 'how the stone ended up under Kingsley's head.'

'He certainly didn't use it as a weapon,' Lem replied.

'Which leads us to the question,' Jeff said,

dismissing the stone as insignificant, 'what happened to the gun?' As he spoke, Jeff moved in that slow, easy way of his toward the massive desk, whose right drawer gaped open. 'From what I've been told, Kingsley owned a Western six-shooter, a Hawes .22 which he kept right here in this desk, fully loaded. And now it's missing.'

'My guess is that the intruder never intended to murder him.' Lem said. 'He sneaked in here thinking he'd rob the place, believing Kingsley was still out of town, and Kingsley surprised him. The robber either knew about Kingsley's gun, or he wrestled it away from Kingsley, shot him and ran.'

'If this is a robbery, then why isn't anything missing?' Kate asked. Kate scanned the study, which revealed fine taste and abundant wealth. Kingsley must have spent a lifetime collecting Western memorabilia. A shiny saddle-set in the corner beneath a tin sign promoting the "Buffalo Bill Cody Wild West Show". Golden spurs, probably having a special history of their own, gleamed from a glass case, along with a rare beaded Indian breastplate, a buckskin shield, and a scattering of spears and arrowheads.

A faded document set in a place of honour to the right of Kingsley's desk. Kate noticed right away that the expensive frame hung at an odd angle. She stepped closer and gave a slight lift to the bottom. The fastening behind the frame had started to break loose, as if someone had attempted to pull it from the wall.

'What do you make of this?' she asked.

'You're looking at the old man's pride and joy,' Lem said, 'an authentic invitation to Tom Horn's hanging. One addressed to Charles Kingsley's grandfather. Kingsley told me himself that this little bit of paper is worth one heck of a lot of money.'

Office of Edwin J. Smalley
Sheriff
Laramie County

Cheyenne, Wyoming,
November 15, 1903

Mr Harold Kingsley,
Laramie, Wyo

Harold Kingsley:
You are requested to be present at the legal execution of Tom Horn which will occur Friday morning at two o'clock, November 20, 1903 at the Laramie County Jail.

E. J. Smalley, Sheriff

'Prep probably hasn't even heard of Tom Horn,' Jeff said smugly. 'Wyoming's hero turned outlaw,' he explained for her benefit. 'He worked as a hired gun for the big cattle barons around here in the late 1800s and early 1900s. Everyone in these parts knows his motto: "killing men is my specialty".'

'Haven't you noticed the way the document is hanging? All the other items are in perfect order, but not this frame.'

'We'll dust it for prints, but if the intruder came here to rob, he was no doubt wearing gloves.' Lem regarded the item for a while in silence. 'I'd say he planned to steal the whole collection, until he laid eyes on Kingsley. He must have known the niece lived here too, and thought that the minute she heard the shots, she would call for help.'

'What's keeping her anyway?' Jeff demanded, glancing at Kate. As if he were the one in charge, he said in his usually overconfident way, 'Your first order of business should be to get a rational statement from the only other person in the house.'

Kate, from the moment Charles Kingsley's niece had admitted them, had been struck with the thought that Kingsley's death might be an inside job. As far as she knew, Charles Kingsley had only one heir, and Kingsley possessed a vast fortune made from land and cattle.

'The best time to grill a suspect is before they've had time to make up a story. Just go up to her room and get her,' Jeff prodded. 'If she has anything to tell, I'll get it out of her.'

'The girl's had a great shock,' Kate replied. 'No matter what she knows, we're going to have to go slowly. If we don't gain her confidence, she'll tell us nothing.'

'You're the boss,' Jeff said sarcastically.

Why couldn't he work with her instead of against her? When she had first joined the office, fresh out of the police academy, she had liked this big man with his all-the-time-in-the-world air and his slow smile. She had often caught him looking at her, as if he approved of her slender form, her suntanned face, her tousled black hair. She had probably been wrong in thinking he would ever do anything but reject her.

Not wanting to argue with him, Kate turned to Lem. Being a newcomer, she didn't know the local families the way he did and that put her at a disadvantage. 'What can you tell me about Kingsley? I've heard rumours that he had a long list of enemies.'

'How right you are,' Jeff spoke up before Lem could reply. 'The one that leaps to

13

mind is his neighbour.'

'You mean the owner of the Double S?'

'Right. Sam Swen, but everyone around here just calls him Swen. The Rocking C and the Double S have been involved in open warfare for years. I heard through the grapevine that Charles Kingsley had just threatened to take Swen to court. Claimed he had proof that Swen was rustling his cattle.'

Rustling cattle — just like the days of the Old West.

'Ah, that's just talk,' Lem scoffed. 'They're both millionaires three times over. Besides, the two of them had been fighting forever. Water rights, range rights — they almost made a game of it. If Swen really wanted Kingsley dead, he'd have killed him years ago.'

Still, a legal battle could be serious business. Kate looked down at the dead man. No testimony, no court case.

'It's the stone under the dead man's head that doesn't fit it,' Kate said at last. 'There's certain to be more to this than a bungled burglary.'

'You may be right there.' Lem's attention had returned to the invitation to Tom Horn's hanging. 'In that legend about Tom Horn, they say that whenever he killed a man, he left behind a kind of signature. He always placed a stone under his victim's head.'

Jeff chuckled. 'Are you saying that Tom Horn's ghost murdered poor Charles Kingsley?'

Not a ghost, Kate thought. Her eyes shifted back to the invitation to Tom Horn's hanging. Had the rare collector's item been what the thief had really been after? If so, why hadn't he taken it? Maybe the invitation to Tom Horn's hanging had never been the cause of the crime, but it must certainly have inspired the killer to put the stone under Kingsley's head as a symbol of vengeance. But who had put the stone there and as vengeance for what crime?

Charles Kingsley's niece, Mary Ellen, stood immobile in the doorway, white knuckled fingers holding talon-like to the doorframe. Her thin body shivered and her narrow face remained lowered, half-obscured by straight dark blonde hair.

Mary Ellen had gone upstairs to change from her robe and slippers. The little-girl image Kate had noticed earlier was now magnified by the pale, flowered blouse and the denim jumper. Kate thought again, as she had when she had first seen her, that

15

most murders are committed by members of the victim's own family. Kingsley's niece, a young woman in her late twenties, the last of the Kingsleys, would likely inherit the whole of the cattle baron's fortune.

Kate glanced at Mary Ellen again and began to doubt her snap judgment. This wispy figure seemed less a cold-blooded killer than some frightened and dependent child.

Jeff didn't notice her shattered condition or didn't care. His tone became gruff, void of that slow drawl he used when addressing Kate. 'We need a full account. Starting with the last time you saw your uncle.'

'That would be at the evening meal. I left right after that and went up to my room.'

'And?'

Mary Ellen's hands gripped the doorframe tighter. She swayed a little and for a moment Kate thought she might faint.

'Three shots.' Her voice fell to a mere whisper. 'They sounded so loud, like cracks of a whip. By the time I had run down the steps, whoever had killed him was gone.'

'You didn't glimpse anyone,' Kate asked gently, 'or hear any scraps of conversation?'

Mary Ellen shook her head. 'The outside door was flung wide open. Uncle Charles was lying on the floor beside his desk.' She drew in her breath sharply. 'Then I saw the blood . . .' Her hands fell to her side, and she took a step backwards.

'Did you call us right away?'

'Yes.'

'You phoned in at eleven fifty-five. That sets the time of death at just before midnight.'

The tears that streamed down her face didn't faze Jeff in the least. 'What happened before that? Did you hear the sound of breaking glass?'

'I didn't.' Mary Ellen's voice caught in a sob, 'I'd been asleep and then those shots sounded. I thought. . . .'

'Thought what?' Jeff demanded.

The girl covered her face with her hands as if about to totally break down.

'Just let me talk to her,' Kate replied, reaching Mary Ellen and ushering her through the hallway to the kitchen. Mary Ellen slumped down at the dining table. Kate busied herself refilling the coffee maker, saddened by the young woman's desolate, whimpering sounds.

Even after the coffee was poured, Kate waited in silence for Mary Ellen to collect herself. She had the most to gain by Charles Kingsley's death, that fact didn't change because of tears. Kate studied her, reminding herself that Mary Ellen's total devastation was as likely to spring from guilt as from grief.

After a while, unprompted by Kate, Mary Ellen said in a small, quiet voice, 'When Uncle Charles returned from Casper, he told me he had got married over the weekend.'

Kate stared at Charles Kingsley's niece, her major suspect altering as she did. Kingsley's hasty marriage, unless he had a prenuptial agreement, would change the main beneficiary of his fortune. 'Whom did he marry? Is she someone you know?'

'Jennie Irwin. I've met her, that's all. Hal Barkley, that's Uncle Charles' foreman, introduced her to him at one of our barbecues last summer. I didn't even know they were dating, so this sudden marriage really took me by surprise.'

'He hadn't even hinted?'

'Not a word. But Uncle Charles was that way. He made his own decisions without considering. . . .' Mary Ellen retreated, changing her last word, 'without ever talking things over with anyone else.'

'What can you tell me about Jennie Irwin?'

'She has a good job as a secretary for Talbart's Insurance in Casper. She lives in an apartment downtown, but I can't tell you the address.'

Kate left to relay the information to Jeff. 'We'll have to contact her before his death is released to the paper,' she said.

Jeff raised his eyebrows as he looked across the room to Lem. 'I didn't know that,' he said sarcastically.

Lem laughed.

With irritation mounting, Kate replied, 'Just see to it that she is contacted at once.'

'Will do,' Jeff drawled with the same air of teasing disrespect.

Lingering anger remained with Kate as she returned to the kitchen. She tried to keep it from sounding in her voice as she asked, 'How did you feel about your uncle's bringing a wife home?'

'Uncle Charles lived alone for so many years. His wife died when he was just starting out in the cattle business. When I was seven years old, Dad was killed in a plane crash, and he took me in. How could I not want him to be happy?'

Her words rang into the silence, sounding for some reason unconvincing.

'So you welcomed the idea? Even though you don't know that much about her.'

'I had expected him to stay in Casper for a few days, so it surprised me when he came back yesterday. He said we had to talk. He

19

wanted me to understand that we could all live here together, but I told Uncle Charles that starting a marriage with someone else in the house was not a good idea. I told him I intended to leave. He argued a while, then said if that was what I wanted, he'd help me find a suitable place.'

'Most people are killed over money,' Kate said, 'in one form or another. My deputy believes this is a simple robbery or robbery attempt. Did Mr Kingsley keep a lot of cash in the house?'

'Not usually.'

'What about his Wild West collection? Even what's displayed behind the desk, the Bill Cody memorabilia, the invitation to Tom Horn's hanging, the breastplate that belonged to a Shoshone chief, all that must be worth quite a lot of money.'

'Some sneak thief could have broken in. If that's what happened, Uncle Charles must have walked in on him.' Mary Ellen stared for a long time at her untouched cup of coffee, then burst out, 'It was probably some thief after cash. I can't believe he was intending to steal those historical items for they would be much too hard to peddle.'

That had a ring of truth, unless the robber had some inside connection. 'But if the intruder intended to rob, I find it strange that he didn't take anything at all. When he didn't find money, it seems he would have taken what he could and run,' Kate said. 'There's something else I find odd, too.' Kate told her about the granite rock, ending with, 'they say Tom Horn always left a stone under the heads of the men he shot. It was his way of tagging his victims so people would know it was one of his kills. Whoever murdered your uncle was mimicking this unusual trademark.'

Mary Ellen took off her glasses. Her large hazel eyes, void of the thick lenses, looked stark and deeply shocked. After a while she put them on again gazing at Kate intently, 'This could be related to Tom Horn,' she said in the same small voice, 'but not in the way you think.'

Kate leaned forward. 'In what way?'

'My uncle has a neighbour, Sam Swen. You've probably heard of him.'

'Yes, the owner of the Double S.'

'The two of them were bitter enemies. Right before he left for Casper, I heard my uncle talking to Swen on the phone. He was very angry. He told Swen he was going to bring charges against him for cattle rustling. That this time he could prove it.'

'But we found no papers concerning any lawsuit.'

21

'It may be at his lawyer's office. He had a big file he was always working on. Swen knew all about it.'

'Then you think,' Kate said, 'that when Mr Kinglsey returned from Casper, Swen might have come to the house to talk things over with him.'

Mary Ellen continued to stare at her in the same startled way. 'They could have fought and Swen could have shot him.' Mary Ellen fell silent for a while. 'But it wouldn't have to have been Swen. He's got a right-hand man who would do anything to protect him, his foreman, Ty Garrison. It's that man who really scared Uncle Charles. It's that man who really scares me.'

Kate drove quickly along the deserted road toward the Double S Ranch.

Evening was fast approaching and a smell of rain wafted in the air. Well-kept pastureland stretched endlessly on either side of her. Cattle, red-gold coats shining in the waning light, milled uneasily, as if aware of an approaching storm. They stopped all motion to watch curiously as she passed.

The road dead-ended just ahead. Across a high wooden arch dangled an iron sign: Double S. Even from this distance Kate could glimpse Swen's house; white, with a columned porch, which would have been more at home on some southern plantation.

A lone man bent on one knee repairing the gate to a huge corral. He wore a black jacket and a dark Stetson obscured his face, causing him to seem more of a shadow than a real person.

As Kate started toward him, the man rose slowly, wiping his hands across long, jean-clad legs. With a hint of a smile, he read aloud the lettering on her badge, 'Belle County Sheriff.' He added jokingly, 'A great improvement over Ben Addison.'

Definitely not Swen, much too young, Kate thought, and handsome in a rugged sort of way. She liked his eyes, the way they had unexpectedly lightened, their colour uncertain in the stormy light.

'What brings the sheriff of Belle County out here?' he asked. As he spoke, he removed his hat, freeing waves of sun-streaked hair. Again she was struck by the attractiveness of his features, chiselled and vigorous, like a Frederick Remington sculpture.

'Have you heard about what happened at the Kingsley ranch last night?'

'Sad business,' he replied with a shake of his head, 'but it has absolutely nothing to do with the Double S.'

'I need to talk to Mr Swen. Is he here?'

'You can talk to me,' he said.

Moments ago she had liked his eyes, but now they had become cold and challenging. Perhaps all the talk about Tom Horn caused the image of an outlaw to spring to her mind, to become one with the man Mary Ellen had warned her about, who could very well be Swen's hired gun.

'I'm foreman of the Double S,' he said, as if he had intercepted her thoughts, 'Ty Garrison. Whatever business you have with Swen, you can discuss with me.'

'Not possible,' she replied.

As Kate continued to stare at him, the outlaw image intensified. What she had at first taken to be a shadow along his jawline, she now recognized as a dark bruise — from a fight. Her thoughts shifted back to the dead man. Ty Garrison could have forced his way into Charles Kingsley's house last night and battled with Kingsley over his gun.

'Someone murdered Charles Kingsley. I need to ask a few questions to Mr Swen, and you.'

'Ask me anything you want to. As for Swen, his lawyer is Milt Sanders. Talk to him.'

'What dealings have you had with the Rocking C recently?'

'No dealings. Ever.'

'Did you leave this ranch after ten o'clock last night?'

'No. I went to bed early. Alone, so don't bother asking me if anyone can verify my whereabouts.'

'It looks as if you've been in a fight,' Kate said cautiously. 'Do you mind telling me how you got that bruise?'

Humour momentarily returned, flickering in his eyes. 'Would you believe me if I told you I ran into a door?'

Knowing the uselessness of talking to him any longer, she started toward the house. Ty Garrison swiftly caught up with her. At the entrance he stepped in front of her, blocking her way. 'I told you, Swen's not available now.'

'Then I will be back.'

Without bothering to reply, he turned, strode across the porch and into the house.

The rudeness of Swen's foreman, the bruise on his face, only served to justify her suspicion that one or both of them might be involved in Kingsley's death. Although Ty Garrison had led her to believe that Swen wasn't home, Kate felt certain that the man she wanted to talk to stood just inside the house, right behind that closed door.

Kate drove off, but had no intention of leaving. She parked the squad car behind a copse of trees near the ranch and hiked back. She headed toward an old shed where, while remaining out of sight, she could watch the front door.

Soon, a figure emerged from the house. Swen walked like a young man, head held high, his steps quick as he crossed the yard to a tan Dodge truck with a showy silver Double S hood ornament. Kate first noted the hardness of his face, his leathery skin cut with deep lines. A man to be reckoned with, she thought.

Before he had a chance to open the truck door, she approached. 'You've heard about Charles Kingsley,' she said.

Swen turned, startled. His heavy denim jacket hung open as if he had thrown it on hastily. Beneath it he wore a flannel shirt, the same faded grey as his eyes. 'Guess his double-dealing finally caught up with him.'

The light that remained in the evening sky glinted in his narrowed gaze. He seemed to be assessing her, labelling her as the enemy.

'I was here earlier. Your foreman told me you were unavailable.'

Swen made no reply.

'Do you know how he got that bruise on his face?'

Still no answer.

'You might as well tell me. You know I'll find out.'

'That fight was between him and Kingsley's foreman. Hal Barkley came over here mouthing off, and Ty showed him the way home. That's all there was to it.'

Recalling Mary Ellen's words, Kate decided to press the issue. 'Ty Garrison has been in trouble with the law before. Did you know that when you made him foreman?'

'I hire cowhands. Not usually from church groups. Ty's top of the line. A bit overprotective, maybe. Has an overdose of loyalty, but believe me, that isn't a fault.'

'Where were you last night, Mr Swen?'

'In my office with the books. Until around midnight when I turned in.'

'Can anyone verify that?'

'No,' he cut her off. 'Why would I be in need of an alibi?' His voice had not risen. His eyes remained level, too. They possessed depth and perception that in some way softened the ruggedness of his appearance; that and the fact that his iron-grey hair curled in such a boyish fashion around his temples.

She decided that he would respond better to frankness. 'You're a major suspect,' she

27

returned. 'You've made threats. I can find witnesses.'

'You go ahead and line up your witnesses,' he said, still unruffled. 'That won't get any further than the other contemptible charges Kingsley was always bringing against me.'

'Cattle rustling, you mean?'

'Why would I want to steal from his straggly old herd? I run top-grade cattle. Truth is, I could buy and sell him.'

'According to statements I got from the Rocking C, Mr Kingsley intended to take you to court. He must have thought he had a solid case against you.'

'He had . . . nothing. Just a set-up attempt. Just another one of his crooked schemes to try to force me out. He always wanted to own the whole blasted territory.'

'Did he say the same thing about you?'

Swen had met her open accusations without taking offence. This statement caused him to react. 'That's your last question,' he replied slowly. 'I've got work to see to.'

'No, I have one more. Have you ever heard of Tom Horn's signature? Of the way he left a stone beneath the heads of the people he gunned down?'

Swen stared at her coldly. 'Everyone around here knows that story,' he said in the same low, controlled tone. 'Horn killed cattle rustlers. Did the law's job, I'd say. He wasn't ashamed of what he did either, or he wouldn't have left that trademark behind, the one I've always called the "stone of vengeance".'

The stone of vengeance — Swen's words kept replaying. Kate tried to concentrate on the rough, winding road that cut across so much empty land, vast rolling hills now encased by darkness. A light drizzle had started to fall, and she turned on her windscreen wipers, enjoying the pleasant rain smell in the air, the methodical slap-slap of the blades against the glass.

She liked driving alone in the squad car, the only part of her busy day that allowed her time to think. Her thoughts locked on the Double S, the double threat that existed there in the form of Sam Swen and Ty Garrison. With Sheriff Addison in the hospital, that meant she must go up against them herself and for a moment she wondered if that were possible.

Kate had sensed about Sam Swen a certain out-manoeuvering shrewdness and that made her wary of him. Not that this trait couldn't be found in honourable men. She couldn't really think of Swen as a cold-blooded killer, yet if Swen thought himself justified, she could well picture him squaring off with his long-time enemy.

But more likely, she qualified, Swen had hired Ty Garrison to do his dirty work for him. Maybe he had employed this drifter as a gun hand, the same way the cattle barons of long ago had hired Tom Horn to rid themselves of rustlers. Swen had even defended Horn to her, pointing out that he had only been doing the law's business.

Kate must find out more about Ty Garrison, what, for instance, lay behind his deep allegiance to Swen. She wondered if Swen had done some favour for him, bailed him out of jail, or got him out of some kind of trouble. How far would Garrison go to prove his loyalty to Swen? Would his job description include murder if he felt it necessary to keep Swen safe?

A sudden curve called her full attention back to the road. She checked her speed; if she had spotted someone else going that fast she would have given them a ticket, she thought wryly. Though she didn't have to worry about encountering any traffic at all out here.

The rain increased, forcing her to slow down further. Kate tensely focused her efforts on trying to steer the vehicle safely through the pelting downpour.

She was approaching an intersection of

two blacktopped roads, which marked the division between the Double S and the Rocking C. Before she reached it, headlights some distance away off to the north, switched on. The sudden glow, penetrating through blackness and pouring rain, alarmed her.

She could make out what she thought to be an old pickup roaring towards her. Cold fear gripped her as she realized that whoever sat behind the wheel planned to collide with her. She attempted to swerve sideways into a stop, but the driver of the truck was closing in on her with madman speed.

CHAPTER 2

Kate strained to see through the rain-drenched window. She couldn't make out the face of the driver, only a wide-brimmed hat pulled low, but for a moment her headlights illuminated a black-clad arm.

Panic filled her. He was going to run her off the road! If she survived the crash, he would find and kill her!

She felt jarred by the shuddering impact of metal against metal. The airbag activated. She struggled with this, trying frantically to maintain her hold on the wheel, but the jolt sent her sliding to the muddy shoulder of the road. The tyres on the right side sank and the vehicle began to spin and roll.

The car slammed to a stop on the passenger side, the one that had taken the brunt of the collision. Kate, stunned, peered from the crazily tilted windscreen in time to see the fast disappearing tail-lights of the truck.

For a moment, Kate remained motionless. She cautiously rotated her shoulder, which had been wrenched during the impact. Nothing more than a dull ache. She moved her right leg. Despite the slight pain, she felt a great sense of relief that nothing was broken. She had survived without serious injury.

Kate battled the airbag and freed herself from the seat belt. The front door would not open. On shaky legs, she worked her way into the back seat and managed to push up the back door. She climbed out into the rain.

She located her police radio and used it to call the station. She would, of course, get Jeff instead of Lem. 'Stay where you are,' he said.

As if she could go anywhere, she thought wryly.

'I know that intersection. I'm on my way.'

The big deputy had never looked so good to her. For the first time since she had known him, he addressed her in a totally earnest way, 'Kate, are you hurt?' He held her against him for a moment. 'You're soaking wet.'

Supporting her, he led her to his car, then hurried to the driver's side and ducked in under the wheel. 'Got to get you to the hospital.'

'No, Jeff. I'm fine. Just a little shaken.'

'Don't give me that. You need to see a doctor.'

'We can't waste any time. Whoever hit me headed off into the canyon area.'

'I've called in the description of the vehicle that you gave me, but I doubt we'll find him. Probably some drunk. Hit and run.'

'No, I was a deliberate target.'

As usual, Jeff didn't listen. 'He must have got scared when he saw he'd hit a cop car. He'll lay low if he's smart, keep the vehicle off the road. Maybe hide it in some garage or barn until he can repair it. Too bad you didn't get any license plate number.'

'Too dark and rainy for that,' Kate said.

Jeff slanted her a close look. 'You sure you're all right?'

Kate nodded.

'Take off that jacket and get into this.' He reached into the back seat and handed her his raincoat. 'I'm going to take a look around.'

Jeff returned. Now that he knew she was unharmed, he became once more the Jeff she knew and didn't love. He gave a low whistle, 'It will have to be towed out.' Jeff shook his head, for a moment seeming more satisfied than sympathetic. 'Our new patrol car. Ben's not going to like this.'

'Did you find anything that would serve as evidence?'

Jeff spoke in his slow, sardonic way, 'No. In fact, I'm going to report that you just made up this speeding truck story. That you ran off the road and tried to cover up your carelessness. Too afraid to face old Ben with all the damage you've done.'

Some time to be tormenting her with his teasing. Kate wasn't even able to work up her usual irritation. She felt lost in the huge raincoat, like a child trying to play sheriff. 'Let's get started. The truck was badly damaged. It's possible it didn't get far away from here. I want to check all the roads he could possibly have taken.'

'You're sure this wasn't just some normal hit and run?'

'I'm positive.'

Jeff often seemed more annoying when he became dead serious. 'Ben should have known better than to have put you in charge,' he said at last. 'He's set you up for this attack. You're no match for some crazy killer. What were you doing out here after hours anyway?'

'I went over to the Double S. I wanted to question Swen.'

'So that's what happened. You crossed the mighty Sam Swen, and he got back at you.'

Kate thought of the glimpse of the driver's arm clad in dark jacket just like the one Ty Garrison had been wearing. 'Maybe not Swen,' she replied, 'but someone is definitely warning me to back off from the Kingsley murder.'

Jeff cut from the old blacktop back to the main highway. 'Where are we going?' Kate asked incredulously. 'The truck headed the other way.'

'I'm taking you to Rock Creek.'

Arguing with Jeff, as always, proved useless. 'Then just drop me off at home,' Kate said as they approached the town. 'I don't need to see a doctor.'

Relieved to be free of Jeff, Kate quickly changed clothes, got in her personal vehicle, and started off on her own search. She spent the next half hour driving through torrents of rain, up and down treacherous and slippery side roads. Kate kept her eyes trained on the pine-covered ravines.

She turned onto a dirt trail, her Landcruiser, despite the four-wheel drive, careening on the soggy surface. The trees that encroached on each side made strange, dripping shadows that looked ghostly in the darkness. Tyres skidded as they laboriously climbed the steep hill flanked by deep gullies. Midway up Kate spotted the black shape of a vehicle left abandoned at the bottom of the embankment.

She couldn't believe her luck — she had found the truck. Kate drove to the level at the top and stopped. With gun in one hand, torch in the other, with feet sliding on the muddy slope, she quickly made her way downward. Even though the indistinct image blended with the blackness, she felt certain this was the truck. The driver, thinking the vehicle would not be found here for some time, had purposely abandoned it; if it had accidentally veered from the shoulder, it would not have ended up on all four wheels.

Rain streamed across the smashed front end of the pickup and dripped from the gap of broken headlight. Kate encircled the truck and to her surprise found a licence plate from Belle County. At the front, halted again and drew in a gasp of surprise when she made out on the twisted plate the gleaming red letters: Double S.

Kate, rain thudding around her, forced open the driver's door. Just as she flashed the beam of light into the cab, she heard the rushing sound of footsteps from behind her. Although she had no time to spin around, she got an impression of a dark-clad arm lifted high in the air. A blow struck the side of her head, causing her to fall forward. Intense pain fingered like fire through the base of her neck and into her shoulders. She tried to pull herself up, to glimpse the face of her attacker, but blackness blotted her vision. Kate groped for some handhold, but felt herself slipping downward into a murky bed of mud and water.

Kate regained consciousness not knowing where she was, but aware of the jolting of a heavy truck. At first she thought she had been dumped into the old pickup, but the dome light shone across a polished dashboard and expensive leather seats. Slowly she made out Ty Garrison's sharp, distinct profile. His broad shoulders leaned forward, large hands intently gripping the wheel.

She brought a hand to her temple, badly swollen, but not bleeding. Shaking from cold and pain, her words sounded unclear, jumbled, 'Where are you taking me?'

Ty Garrison didn't need to answer for they were already passing under the Double S sign and heading toward Swen's house.

Fear increased the throbbing in her temple. Her gun, if Ty hadn't picked it up, lay in the mud near the abandoned pickup. Helplessness gripped her, making her feel like a prisoner being dragged before some pitiless judge.

Swen, alerted by their approach, stepped outside. He waited under the cover of the huge, circular porch. Rain drummed against the roof and poured from the overhang. Kate could barely make out his words. 'I thought you'd be in the hospital. What are you doing out in this storm?'

'She found the vehicle that wrecked her squad car,' Ty replied. 'Not far from here, on our land. She must have pulled up before the driver had a chance to get away. She's been hurt.'

'Hurt? How?'

'I was struck from behind. I never saw who hit me.'

'Let's get her inside.'

Kate, allowing Ty to assist her, leaned against him. Swen led them into a cosy room where high bookshelves towered between a huge stone fireplace. The lapping warmth of flames battled against her reluctance and fear.

Swen quickly left the room.

'How did you find me?' Kate asked. 'What were you doing out there?'

'I began to search the minute we got the

call about the wreck,' Ty said. 'But don't try to talk now. Let me see how badly you're hurt.'

Swen returned with a towel and a pan of water. Ty carefully cleaned the wound, then gently wiped the mud from her face. 'She's got to get into some dry clothes,' he said. 'Do you have something she can wear?'

In Swen's room Kate changed into faded jeans and a shirt sizes too large for her. She had stopped shivering by the time she returned to the fireplace.

Swen was talking on the phone. 'Ty found our truck, the one that maniac used to crash into the patrol car. Sheriff Jepp is injured, but not seriously. She's here at the Double S.'

When he hung up, he remained seated, his hand still on the phone. 'Ty filled me in on all that's happened. You've got real spunk, kid,' he added with a slight smile. 'I've been kicking around the notion of offering you a job.'

Ty with the same look of approval handed Kate a cup of hot coffee. She took a bracing drink, wondering how in such a short time she could be feeling safe and comforted.

'I'm going to need all the help I can get,' Swen said. 'I knew the minute I heard about that fool "stone of vengeance" left at the crime site, that I was being set up. And now this. You can see what Kingsley's killer is trying to do to me.'

'The rustling started about three years ago,' Ty explained. 'All this time both Swen and I have believed Kingsley was stealing our cattle just for spite. But we had another incident this afternoon. A fence broken, several animals missing.'

'Hal Barkley is a scoundrel,' Swen chimed in, 'but without Kingsley behind him, he wouldn't have the guts to keep stealing on his own.' Swen's voice lowered, blending with the sound of crackling flames. 'That's why I'm beginning to have second thoughts.'

'What thoughts?' Kate asked.

'The rustler may have been targeting both ranches all along,' Ty answered for him, 'knowing both of us would blame the other. He, in fact, may not be associated with either the Rocking C or the Double S. But whoever he is, we intend to track him down.'

'We're willing to work with you, Kate,' Swen declared. 'Together we'll catch that thief, the man who murdered Kingsley.'

Kate glanced from one to the other again. If the Double S were involved, it made little sense that they would use one of their own trucks to crash into her car. Ty wouldn't have shown up on the scene to help her either, and under no circumstances would he have brought her here. Despite all of today's problems, she had at least made some progress: she was gaining the confidence of two very capable men. 'What would you suggest we do?'

'I have a little plan,' Swen said, leaning forward. 'And I've half a mind to let you in on it.'

There couldn't have been a worse moment for Jeff to burst into the room. He stood at the entrance, uniform soaked, water making trails through his hair and across his face. Some time for him to show up, at just the moment Swen and Ty planned to confide in her. She could tell by Jeff's aggressive attitude that he was going to ruin everything.

'So you found the truck,' he said, pointing an almost accusing finger at Kate. 'And Garrison just happened to be on hand. Why didn't you take her to the hospital?'

'Because we were very close to this ranch. And I didn't need to go. I'm perfectly all right, Jeff.'

Jeff stepped belligerently forward, hands on his hips. 'The vehicle belongs to the Double S. How do you explain that? Your foremen had no trouble at all locating this pickup, even though our entire patrol unit failed to find it. Just what do you say to that?'

'I'd say you're lucky,' Swen drawled, 'that Ty found her when he did.'

'You have some real explaining to do, Swen!'

Swen's features tightened, became hard and tough. 'What's there to explain? This is a frame-up. I've been set up.'

'Did you give anyone permission to drive your truck this evening?'

'Of course I didn't. Someone stole my pickup to incriminate me. It would be easy enough to do. I always keep it parked out by the barn.'

The room fell silent. The fire in the grate had died down and left only the storm outside, the billowing wind and the sound of splashing water.

'Swen leaves the keys in the ignition,' Ty's manner became as hostile as Jeff's.

'Why's that?'

'So the hands can use it anytime without bothering me,' Swen replied.

'Jeff, I've got their statements,' Kate cut in, 'no need to go over the details again.'

'I want to hear them myself.'

Angrily Kate rose. Jeff was deliberately alienating people who were in a position to help them. Not to mention the fact that he

43

was openly challenging her authority.

All trace of cooperation drained from Swen's voice. 'What do you think we'd gain by rigging this accident? We have no reason to harm Kate.'

Jeff continued to stare at Ty, although he addressed Swen. 'Someone, maybe someone you hire, might not want Kingsley's death investigated.'

Ty stepped forward. 'Just be careful. Don't think you can come here and make accusations you can't back up.'

Jeff glared at Ty's clenched fist. 'What? Do you plan to attack me, too, just like you did Kingsley's foreman?'

'Don't believe any of that nonsense Hal Barkley told you,' Swen said acidly. 'He came over here in a rage, accusing us of cutting a fence line, of letting our cattle run with his. You know how mean he gets. Ty did what he had to do.'

'Doesn't quite sound like the story Barkley told me,' Jeff said. 'Come on, Kate.' Jeff started away, then swung back. 'We had your pickup taken to Rock Creek for the lab to go over.'

'Fine,' Ty responded coldly. 'You're not going to find proof that anyone from the Double S was driving that truck tonight.'

'Then I'd say,' Jeff returned, 'that we're

looking at one very strange coincidence.'

Glad to have the office to herself, Kate sat alone in the evidence room, the items found in Swen's black pickup spread on the wooden table before her. She studied the contents taken from the cab. Expected items had been stuffed in the glove compartment: registration, statements from the co-op and from feed stores, a tattered map of Belle County.

She lifted the clip-on earring that had been found crushed on the floorboard of the truck. Mud mashed into the intricate beadwork of a lovely Sioux design. Black background and red and blue beads made a unique geometric pattern. The Indian style reminded her of Charles Kingsley's love for the Wild West.

The leather backing looked relatively new which caused her to discard the idea that the beadwork was part of the Kingsley collection. But it was expensive, and pricey jewellery like this was usually sold as a set.

Jeff didn't believe it had been lost by the driver of the pickup, but Kate had her doubts. A woman might have been behind the wheel. The earring could, in fact, belong to Mary Ellen Kingsley.

If Kate asked her outright, she would get

only a denial. Moreover, finding the owner wouldn't necessarily prove any connection to the crime. Kate decided to keep this evidence confidential for the time being, hoping that she might locate a matching bracelet or necklace.

The department's spare vehicle looked almost as battered as the squad car Kate had wrecked. Still, it had wheels and a motor, which was all that Kate needed to take her back to the scene of the crime.

After visiting the Double S, she saw Kingsley's vast, sprawling estate with new eyes. The towering house appearing in hazy glimpses through thick branches, had been modernized throughout the years. Even the huge gazebo and the columned porch, whitewashed and impressive, seemed added on as if in competition to Swen, as if the men were playing some kind of Western version of 'keeping up with the Joneses.'

Back at the office she had checked the phone records: the 3 p.m. callphone call Kingsley had made to Mary Ellen to tell her of his marriage, the 3.45 p.m. call Mary Ellen made to the Belle County Museum. Kingsley had arrived at the house about 7.30 p.m. on Monday. Unusual for him, he parked his truck in the garage, maybe to make carrying items inside easier. The only clear tracks were from his vehicle. Of course the driveway that enclosed the garden and gazebo were of blacktop.

Kate glanced towards the gazebo. Lacework, pale and delicate, decorated the sides. The small structure rose high in the air, suspended on stately, stilt-like braces.

As Kate half-circled the gazebo, her attention was caught by a fresh upheaval of earth on the side hidden both from the house and from the main road. No reason for anyone to be digging under there. Strange Lem and the boys who had gone over the yard hadn't noticed that this small area, about the size of a revolver, had been disturbed. With pounding heart, thinking she might have found where the killer had disposed of the murder weapon, Kate hurried toward it.

Kneeling, feeling soreness from last night's wreck, she began scooping away the loose soil. The ground soon became solid against her fingers, impossible without a tool to dig. Her excitement died as quickly as it had flared: she had discovered nothing.

Rising, wiping her hands against the legs of her uniform, she looked up, facing the curious glances of hired men loitering near the corral. She started toward them. Of the four, only one looked friendly enough to address. 'Is Hal Barkley around?'

'In there,' he answered, waving an arm toward the barn.

Kate, glad to be putting distance between her and the Rocking C's rough-looking cowhands, hurried toward the old-fashioned barn, recently painted a dark red. She passed through the open doors into the dimness, heavy with the scents of horses, of hay and grease.

Eyes adjusting to the changing light, she halted. The last thing she had expected was to find Charles Kingsley's foreman with a woman in his arms.

'Mr Barkley,' Kate said, her voice resounding in a loud, startled way.

Almost guiltily, the two broke apart. If this were some stolen moment of love, Kate saw no evidence of it on the woman's face which registered, not joy, but stark pain.

Hal Barkley's burly arms dropped to his side. He stepped forward threateningly, as if all of his battles were physical ones. In the background, the woman wiped at her tears.

'Just what kind of department are you running, anyway?' he demanded.

Light from the door caught his features, the generous nose, the bearded chin. Many women might find his aggressive maleness attractive, despite the slight beer gut that strained his tight t-shirt and the fact that he probably had the brains of a moose.

'You should have done your job!' Barkley accused. 'No one notified poor Jennie of Charles' death! She drove out here yesterday morning, all smiles, expecting to make plans for her honeymoon and instead she's planning a funeral!'

'You weren't contacted?' Kate asked, astounded.

'She had to hear it from me!' He hit his fist against his open palm. 'This senseless blunder never would have happened if Ben were the one in charge!'

Kate shouldn't have turned the job of contacting Kingsley's new bride over to Jeff. 'I'm sorry you had to find out like this,' she said sincerely.

'Sorry?' Barkley boomed, taking another step forward.

Jennie placed a restraining hand on his arm. 'I borrowed a car from my friend. No one would have been able to find me, Hal.' Her voice caught in her throat, caused her to stop and dab at tears. 'Out of the blue, I just decided to drive down here and surprise him.'

Kate liked the way she didn't place blame. Using a car with different licence plates, no wonder Jeff hadn't been able to contact her once she had left Casper. Still if Jeff hadn't put his work off, he could have reached her before she got on the road.

'When did you leave home?'

'After Charles left, I got to thinking I should have gone with him. So, on impulse, I decided to find some way over here.'

Jennie Irwin Kingsley, his bride of one day, wasn't at all what Kate had expected. She had imagined some cheap, brassy gold-digger with dyed hair and calculating manner. Jennie's natural beauty, her honey-blonde hair and frank, soft-blue eyes took Kate by surprise. To coin a couple of old clichés, she looked as nice as pie and wholesome as whole wheat bread. If Kate could depend on looks not being deceiving.

Kate turned to Barkley, saying, 'I heard that you and Ty Garrison got into a fight at Swen's ranch.'

'So you're here to arrest me for that.' Barkley advanced from the shadows, stopping only a foot or so from her. Sunlight played across the cuts and bruises that marked his face, the dark ring of black that encircled his left eye.

'No one's pressed any charges. But I do want to hear your account of what happened.'

'In the first place, Swen and that hired gun of his are lying.'

'So far, I haven't even told you what they said.'

Barkley, waving away Kate's remark, raged on, 'I stopped by to let them know they were to fix that fence between our properties. And what happens? Swen sets his hired thug on me. Ty Garrison attacked me!'

'He claims you started the fight.'

'His word against mine. They want that fence down so it's easier for them to steal our cattle.'

'Our records report stolen cattle from both ranches,' Kate said.

'A cover-up. Swen's stealing from us, all right!'

'Would you give me a statement as to your whereabouts Monday, after you left their ranch until the time Mr Kingsley was shot?'

'I left Swen's about seven, went into town, had a few beers at the Lazy Z. After that I headed directly to my house.'

'Can anyone back that up?'

'What do you think?' he answered gruffly. 'I live alone, ten miles down that road north of here.'

Kate studied Barkley. He didn't have an alibi, but then he didn't have much of a motive, either. If Swen had been murdered, it would have been a different story, but Barkley worked for Kingsley and the Rocking C.

'Mr Barkley, what do you know about the lawsuit your employer was intending to bring against Swen?'

He shrugged. 'We've been missing cattle for several years, but as of late, it's getting worse. Old Swen's behind this, you can bet on that. He's been stealing our calves and re-branding our cattle. He does it because he hates Charles, it's game to him. And he's slick. Until recently, we've been unable to make any case against him.'

'What evidence did Mr Kingsley have against Swen?'

'He didn't tell me,' Barkley said.

'Since you're his foreman, why didn't he share this information with you?'

'Charles said he had proof positive. He would have told me all about it if he'd had a chance. If Swen or his hired hitman hadn't sneaked in and murdered him.'

Kate's gaze strayed from Barkley's tough, bearded face to Jennie. As she did, she felt a jolt as she noticed her expensive, Western-style earrings, long loops decorated with diamonds and turquoise. In spite of her wholesome appearance, Jennie, now Kingsley's direct heir, loomed as the one most likely to have killed him. Moreover, Hal Barkley's embrace had seemed to Kate much more than an expression of sympathy and comfort.

'Mrs Kingsley, I'd like to have a word with you. Why don't we go into the house?'

'I'll come with you,' Barkley interceded.

'No need to,' Jennie told him. 'I'll be all right.

'I'm just Jennie, to everyone,' she said as they walked toward the towering house. Jennie, as if the place had always been hers, led Kate into the kitchen. In an almost automatic gesture of hospitality, she drew out Ironstone mugs, filled them with coffee, and slid one forward.

'This has really thrown me,' she said, sinking down across from Kate and absently stirring her coffee.

'It's a terrible shock, I know,' Kate replied. 'What are your plans now?'

Jennie looked up as if the question surprised her. 'Why, I intend to just go ahead and move in. I've already quit my job and given up my apartment. I can manage the ranch, I guess, with Hal's help.'

'What about Mary Ellen?'

'She tells me she will be leaving as soon as possible. I know this has been her home since childhood, and she's welcome to stay until she finds a suitable place.' Jennie stirred her coffee, staring at the black liquid morbidly. 'I'm alone, again. Alone, forever.'

In the stillness Kate thought of Hal Barkley.

'No other man will ever measure up to Charles.'

'What made you decide to make an unexpected trip to Rock Creek?'

'Charles intended for us to go together, but after he talked to Mary Ellen on the phone, he suddenly changed his mind. Probably he wanted the chance to talk things over with her in person when I wasn't on the scene. But I should never have let him go alone. You knew, didn't you, that Charles had a chronic heart problem? The doctors told him that considering his overall health, they had done all they could do for him. He had a year to live, or maybe two, at best.' Jennie looked up suddenly, looped earrings swaying with the quick movement of her head. Kate couldn't help noticing they were the clip-on type, just like the single earring found in Swen's truck. 'I told him I would marry him anyway. I wanted all the time he had left, to make him happy.'

'I didn't know.' Kate waited solemnly watching as Jennie wiped her eyes. Then, thinking of the driver of the black pickup, she said, 'So you arrived at the ranch yesterday.'

'Yes.'

'Can anyone verify the time you left Casper?'

'My friend, Ann Lectie will. I borrowed her car. I was going to start right out, but waited until Tuesday morning. I got here about eleven.'

'I'm puzzled, then, why my office couldn't get in touch with you.'

'Probably because I wasn't home. One thing came up, then another, and they certainly couldn't have found me on the road driving Ann's car.'

Her friend would no doubt supply Jennie with an alibi, would say whatever Jennie wanted her to, still Kate wrote down her name and address, asking as she did, 'How do you think Mary Ellen took the news of Mr Kingsley's marrying?'

'I don't know. Charles avoided discussing his plans with her. Of course, he seldom sought anyone's approval, just went ahead and did what he thought best. He had that "plunge ahead" trait, that's what made him so successful.'

'You would think he'd talk something this important over with her.'

'He wanted to smooth things over with her, that's why he was so set on seeing her on Monday. He had put it off as long as he could, but I understood. He had his

55

reasons.'

'What were they?'

'Charles took Mary Ellen into his home, befriended her and protected her, not that she ever appreciated it. Charles told me when she was sixteen, she fell for some no good drifter who really had his eye on Charles' money. Charles had to step in and run him off. He told me that Mary Ellen never forgave him for that.'

'But you didn't discuss your marriage plans with Mary Ellen, either.'

'I could never get close to her,' Jennie confessed. 'I tried, but she shut me right out from the beginning. Maybe that's her way. She just doesn't know how to act, how to dress, how to talk to people. No one taught her, I suppose. Things might have been different if Charles' first wife hadn't died so young. What Mary Ellen needed was a mother, but that role my handsome cowboy just couldn't play.' Jennie paused, and Kate thought she detected some hint of dislike in her voice. 'The girl's all grown up now, grown up plain and awkward and completely set in her ways.'

At that moment Mary Ellen appeared at the kitchen door. Kate uncomfortably set aside her coffee. Mary Ellen just stood toying with her unattractive glasses. Without them, her eyes looked wide and void of all emotion. Regardless, Kate knew that Mary Ellen had heard Jennie's words. She could tell by the way Mary Ellen kept her eyes fastened on Charles Kingsley's bride.

Jennie, reacting in an embarrassed way, said, 'Poor Charles. Why would anyone want to kill such a wonderful man?'

'For money,' Mary Ellen replied, her voice distant and hollow.

Jennie uneasily went on with her lament. 'He was so kind and thoughtful. Such a wonderful, caring man.'

'He never cared about me,' Mary Ellen said shortly.

Astonished, both Kate and Jennie looked toward her.

'He never, ever, listened to me,' Mary Ellen said with deep, heartfelt resentment. 'He never once considered what I wanted.'

'How can you say that?'

Mary Ellen continued to glare at Jennie, like some defiant teenager. Jennie stared back, the kind aura slowly vanishing. Kate could feel the clash between them, strong and ugly, like the one between Ty and Hal Barkley.

Jennie slowly rose and in a hushed voice, said, 'I'm going down to Charles' study.'

Mary Ellen watched her leave. 'Why

would Uncle Charles marry someone like *her?*' she moaned. 'He objected to the man I loved, but he couldn't hold a candle to her. He never once stepped out on me behind my back, the way Jennie Irwin did to my uncle.'

'Was Jennie seeing someone besides Charles?' Kate asked, not quite believing it, but at the same time thinking about finding Jennie in Hal Barkley's arms. When Mary Ellen didn't respond, Kate prompted, 'Who is he? Do you know?'

'I'm not sure. Why don't you ask her?' Without another word, Mary Ellen whirled around and fled from the kitchen.

In the study Kate found Jennie slumped dejectedly in the huge leather chair behind Kingsley's desk.

'Charles and I first met in this very room,' she said. 'Hal introduced us, and we both fell head over heels.'

Tears filled her eyes again. Either she was truly grieved, or a very good actress. Kate wanted to enquire about the possibility of some man other than Charles Kingsley in her life, but couldn't bring herself to do so. Because of her own grief Mary Ellen had no doubt just been lashing out. Jennie seemed genuinely heartbroken; a sensitive woman, who had about her an air of in-

nocence the shade of her rose-coloured lip-
stick.

Jennie looked around despairingly. 'The
robber must have thought Charles was still
in Casper,' she said. 'No one would break
into his house with him here.'

'You're probably right,' Kate replied, then
added, 'that is, if it were his intention to rob
the house.'

'What else could it be?' Jennie swung
sideways in the swivel chair and faced
Charles Kingsley's Western collection.
'There's motive enough for theft right here
in this very room. Do you have any idea
what this collection is worth?'

'Not actually. What do you think?'

'A fortune, that's what,' Jennie exclaimed,
'but worth more to me than anyone else.
We spent many happy hours browsing
antique shops, looking for treasures to add
to his collection.' Her grave gaze shifted to
the wall. 'That invitation to Tom Horn's
hanging was what he loved most. More than
me, even,' she added with a small smile. 'It
is priceless.'

Kate studied the handwritten invitation,
in perfect condition except for a tiny crease
mark in the far, left corner. The handwrit-
ing was smooth and flowing, as if the sheriff
had given it his best. The tiny ink spot over

the 'i' where the ink had run gave it a human touch.

'It's certainly one of a kind,' Jennie told her. 'Charles said that he knew people who would kill for it. Maybe he was right.'

From the unstable way the invitation was hanging, Kate wondered once again if the intruder had attempted to yank it from the wall. Nothing, Kate thought, would have prevented the robber from snatching it as he ran off. Then why hadn't he taken it? Despite the fact that Kate couldn't answer that question, the Tom Horn invitation had remained stuck in her mind from the very first time she had laid eyes on it.

Kate silently regarded this unusual relic. Yes, such a rare and valuable item could indeed be a motive for murder. One flaw, though, existed in that theory: the invitation to Tom Horn's hanging still hung safe and sound on the wall behind Kingsley's desk.

CHAPTER 3

Sheridan Wallace leaned back in his chair, his mild voice dying away and leaving only the sounds of traffic from the busy street below them. 'I'm sorry I can't be of more help.'

The attorney lacked both the force of the Rocking C's foreman, Hal Barkley, and the vital energy that Kingsley must have possessed. In fact Kate wondered how this aged man with his pale, solemn face had been able to attract such a wealthy client.

The attorney spoke again in his quiet manner. 'Charles called me late Thursday from Casper. He said he had some very urgent business that we needed to discuss. Of course I asked him what it concerned, and he told me that he had finally found enough proof to link Sam Swen with his missing cattle.'

'But he didn't tell you what evidence?'

'I assumed it would consist of documents,

perhaps involving brand tampering and cattle sales. Instead of bringing criminal charges though, I believe he wanted to pursue a civil suit against Swen. But those are only speculations. Unfortunately, I never found out. We spoke our last words to one another that Thursday evening.'

'You have possession of his final will, don't you?' Kate asked.

'Yes. I've already spoken to both Jennie Kingsley and Mary Ellen Kingsley.' His thin lips stretched into the semblance of a smile. 'There's going to be none of those dramatic "reading of the will" scenes that you see on TV.'

'Because he was murdered,' Kate told him, 'I need to know the provisions.'

'Of course. About a month ago Charles Kingsley came into my office. He often made snap decisions and never gave them a second thought. He had made such a decision that day.'

'Concerning his will, you mean?'

'Charles said he wanted to leave everything, all of his real and personal property to Jennie, then Jennie Irwin. I asked him if it were his intention not to mention his niece. You know Mary Ellen is the last of the Kingsleys.'

'What did he say?'

' "We just don't need any bookwork as far as Mary Ellen is concerned." Those were his exact words. He stated that he intended to handle the finances between them himself.' Wallace paused significantly. 'I didn't know about his marriage plans at the time, nor did he tell me.' He gave another of his strained smiles. 'I never make it a practice to interfere. I simply drew up the papers as he requested.'

'Is the will solid?'

'Now that Jennie Irwin has become Jennie Kingsley, it is very definitely solid. Of course, it would have been even had they not married. He was under no obligation to provide for his niece. It is clear that Charles did what he wanted to with his money. His competence is not in question.'

Kate wandered to the window and gazed down at Rock Creek's old buildings, feeling for a moment the same jolt Mary Ellen must have felt upon hearing the news. 'It's hard to believe he left everything to Jennie. Why do you suppose he did that?'

'I never met Jennie until she came into my office after Charles died. Still I could tell he was very much taken with her.' Wallace hesitated, falling into a pensive silence. 'I don't want you to get the wrong idea of Charles,' he said at last. 'He was thoughtful and generous, perhaps to a fault.'

Kate watched the slow movement of the cars along the street. 'Would Mr Kingsley have any special reason to disinherit his niece?'

Sheridan Wallace gave a short laugh, as dry as his smile had been, indicating that he found the idea of Mary Ellen's displeasing anyone preposterous. 'If you want my opinion, Charles intended to give Mary Ellen her inheritance at the same time that he married. Too bad he didn't have the chance to carry out his plans.'

Kate turned back to him. 'How did Mary Ellen take the news?'

'It's hard to tell with someone as private as Mary Ellen. And of course, there were my own feelings. I felt very sorry for her. After all, she has lived at the Rocking C almost all her life, and it did look as if Charles had done this out of pure spite — which, I assure you, wasn't the case.' He folded veined hands in front of him on the desk. 'All in all, I'd say she took it well enough.'

Traffic from the street below encroached into the silent room, and with it an image of Mary Ellen and the resentful — almost vindictive — way she had faced Jennie at the ranch.

64

'Mary Ellen said herself that her uncle owed her absolutely nothing, that she had already received her benefits.' The lawyer went on, 'You've heard the story about how Charles took her in, how he doted on her, giving in to her every wish.'

'How old was Mary Ellen when her family died?'

'I'm not sure, four or five, maybe. All I'm certain of is that it was very hard for him. Charles never had any children around, then here he was faced with the prospect of raising one all alone and a little girl to boot.'

'He didn't legally adopt her?'

'No. No need to. Her mother's family had not the least bit of interest in her so there was no one to contest her living with him.'

'Do you know anything about Mary Ellen's first love? The one Mr Kingsley refused to let her marry?'

'I didn't know him, don't even recall Charles mentioning him by name, only . . .' he added with a small, tight smile, 'by tags. Which, doubtlessly, were right on the mark. But all of that was a long time ago, water under the bridge.'

'I want to thank you, Mr Wallace, for talking to me today.'

After another of his solemn pauses, he said, 'I'll tell you just what I told Mary Ellen. I'm sure Charles didn't intend to cut her off without a cent. From what I always believed, she was as dear to him as any daughter could be.'

Kate reached the door. 'One more thing, what do you know about Mr Kingsley's foreman, Hal Barkley?'

'Very loyal,' the attorney assured her. 'Charles had implicit faith in him. It's a good thing, now wouldn't you say? Jennie Kingsley is certainly going to need his help.'

Kate returned to the Rocking C where she had left Lem sorting through Charles Kingsley's papers. He didn't bother to look up, but said in a disgruntled way, 'We're batting a zero all around.'

Kingsley's desk was piled high with years and years of paperwork. Exact and orderly, Kingsley had kept perfect records. Kate scanned the carefully marked folders: Co-op, Pauley's Auction, Krady's Feed Store. Lem lifted one of them and without a word passed it across to her. This file, labelled neatly with a black marker, read *Swen — Double S.*

'It's empty.'

'You don't sound surprised. I thought a police academy gal like you would believe that all crimes leave paper trails.'

Ignoring the barb, Kate asked, 'Have you

gone through everything?'

'Two more file drawers to go, but what you've got in your hand is all we're going to find.'

'I wonder why anyone would leave the folder and take the contents.'

'Who knows?'

'Have you searched through his vehicles?'

'Nothing in them. And I asked Mrs Kingsley if he had shown her any of his personal records or if he had brought any of them with him to Casper. Both negative.'

A thorough search of the rest of the office brought the same result. Wearily, Kate rose from the chair she had drawn up beside Lem. She checked her watch: almost noon. She had time to visit Ben at the hospital before paying her respects at the cemetery.

'Go on. I'll stay here and put this place back together.' Lem stood up, gathering folders. 'I'm beginning to think the same as Jeff,' he said, 'that Swen's our man.'

'I thought you believed this was a simple robbery.'

'It's still a robbery. Swen broke in to steal the only record of Kingsley's lawsuit.' Lem words were followed by a long, accusing silence. 'We should listen to Jeff more. Jeff's usually right.'

Clearly Lem meant, 'you should listen to

Jeff more,' not 'we should.' He had made this statement just to oppose her. That was obvious by the way his eyes narrowed, and the lines in his thin face tightened. Lem, not willing to discuss this any further, was openly defying her. Disappointed in him, feeling alone in her investigation, she turned away.

Lem's words drifted after her as she crossed to the door. 'Turning up empty-handed here gives us our biggest clue. Swen fought with Kingsley over the lawsuit, shot him, and destroyed the incriminating evidence.'

Kate left and headed for the hospital. Walking down the quiet corridor toward Sheriff Addison's room, Kate recalled what Jeff had said to her at the office last Friday, before Ben became ill.

'I'm busy working on my movie script,' he had drawled. 'Ever heard of that old TV show, "Jake and the Fat Man"? Well, I'm calling this one "Jeff and the Fat Man".'

'Very clever. If it hadn't already been written.'

'Not like this, it hasn't.' Jeff had laughed. 'We're not going to solve crimes. We're just going to hang out at the doughnut shop.'

Jeff's constant jibes often zeroed in on Ben's weight problem, references like that one or his calling Sheriff Addison, 'Sheriff Addapound'. Kate liked those remarks no more than she did his constant teasing about her fancy Criminal Justice degree, which as of late was occurring more often. At least Jeff didn't discriminate: he resented anyone who had any kind of authority over him.

Ben tolerated the ribbing good-naturedly. True, Ben weighed in heavy, but in other ways too. A person could trust what he said — a fair man who didn't play favourites or belong to the good old boy's club.

Kate's friend, affable as ever, sat up in bed his heavy face glowing with joy at seeing her.

'You're looking great,' Kate placed the flowers beside his bed.

'No candy?' he asked with feigned disappointment. 'Just as well. On top of everything, I'm having an ulcer flare-up. Doc's taken me off coffee and everything else I like.'

'But I've talked to your doctor,' Kate said. 'Instead of surgery he may only recommend a long rest. He thinks your symptoms are caused by stress and overwork.'

'The long, tedious hours and the pressures of the job I hand over to you. Pull up a chair, Kate. Jeff told me all about your visit to Swen's and what happened afterwards. But I want to hear it all from you.'

She told him, finishing by saying, 'Whoever shot Kingsley drove that truck straight into the squad car.'

'Jeff said it was registered to Swen's Double S and that you had just left there. What does that tell you?'

'Anyone familiar with the ranch would know they could take this pickup without anyone paying much attention.' She paused. 'Actually, I think the truck was stolen so Swen would be blamed.'

'Maybe that's what he wants you to think. What about the lab report?'

'A beaded earring was found on the floor, one with a geometric Indian design. That could be an important clue.'

'Maybe, maybe not,' Ben said. 'Swen told Jeff the truck was used by his ranch hands and house staff to run errands. The earring could have belonged to someone's wife or girlfriend who had gone along for a ride into town. Doesn't necessarily mean whoever lost it was involved in what happened Tuesday night. Still, earrings come in pairs. It wouldn't hurt to check around, see if you can find out who that one belonged to.'

'As expensive as it is, it's certain to be part of a set,' Kate told him. 'If the owner doesn't know where she lost the earring, she may not dispose of a matching necklace or bracelet. I plan to keep quiet about it and keep my eyes open.'

'Why do you think you were attacked as soon as you reached the abandoned truck?'

'Maybe the driver had just left the vehicle when I pulled up and had to hide. I was struck so he could get away.'

'Or this "he or she" missed some incriminating evidence left behind and decided to return for it.'

Ben was admitting the possibility that the driver was a woman. 'Then why was the earring still there?'

'Because Garrison arrived on the scene, too.'

'I don't know,' Kate said uncertainly. 'I think it was either lost during the wreck and not noticed at the time, or else it was planted.'

'What about fingerprints?'

'Nothing on the steering wheel. Both Swen and Garrison's prints were found in the cab. Ben, what do you think of those two men? I know you've had trouble with both of them before this.'

'Swen has plagued me ever since I swore the oath,' Ben replied. 'I don't know much about Garrison, but Jeff did a rundown on

71

him. He's spent time in jail for brawling at some tavern. But that was years back.'

'Do you think Swen hired him for any special reason?'

'Swen watches his back for sure,' the sheriff stated. 'Just before I got ill, he came to see me about the stealing Kingsley kept accusing him of doing.'

'Jeff and Lem are convinced Swen is the rustler,' Kate said, 'but I'm not. With all of his money, why would he want to do that?'

'For the same reason witches stick pins in dolls,' Ben replied. 'Anyway Kate, I'm glad you came in today.' The smile vanished from his face, causing a sag to his lips that made him look stern. 'Don't go out to the Double S alone again. Take Jeff or Lem as backup. I want this clearly understood. You're not to go against my direct order.'

'If it will make you happy,' she returned lightly.

'By the way, how are you getting along with my two wayward deputies? Are they giving you any trouble?'

Kate thought about how Jeff had not carried out her immediate orders to locate Jennie Kingsley, about the look on Lem's face as he had sided with Jeff. Ben's two deputies were constantly pitted against her, but she did not say anything.

Ben chuckled at her silence. 'They're good boys. Just cut them some slack.'

Kate rose to leave.

'Guess they're burying poor Charles Kingsley about now.' Ben gave a weary sigh. 'If I weren't laid up here, I'd be going to his funeral.'

'I'm stopping by the cemetery.'

'Thanks, Kate. We need to have someone from our office there.'

Ben lifted a white carnation from the vase, sniffed it, then put it back with the others, saying remorsefully, 'This is a real tragedy. Rock Creek has lost a very important member of the community. I only wish I knew why.'

'Money, in one form or another,' Kate replied. 'But what form I'm not sure of yet.'

At the cemetery, people continued to pour from a long line of cars. Kate descended the grassy slope, made her zigzagging way through the vast crowd, and stood alone close to the tent by the new grave.

Grief-stricken friends and neighbours waited near the hearse for the removal of the casket. On their faces Kate read varied emotions: disbelief, apprehension, anger. Sadness seeped over her. She hadn't met Charles Kingsley, yet it was easy to conclude that he was greatly honoured, respected —

yes — even loved by the community.

A heavy-set woman standing near Kate kept whispering to her friend. 'That's the wife. Didn't know what to think when I heard he married so quickly. Do you know her?'

'They say she's from Casper.'

Both women studied Jennie critically.

'She's certainly not what I expected.'

The large woman beside Kate whispered again, 'Still it seems a shame. She'll just step in and take over. Poor little Mary Ellen.'

Kate could see Jennie Kingsley from the open door of the limousine, huddled in the back seat crying. She shook her head when they wanted to help her. She probably would have stayed there, had not Hal Barkley strode forward, bent and extended his hand to her. His raspy voice sounded loud in the surrounding quietness. 'You have to be brave, Jennie. It will soon be over.'

Jennie allowed him to assist her from the vehicle. She leaned heavily on his arm as they made their slow way to the funeral tent. As Jennie passed Kate, she stopped. 'Thanks for being here, Kate,' she said tearfully, 'you're so very kind.' Hal Barkley, looking uncomfortable in his dark, ill-fitting suit, served as one of the pallbearers. Kate recognized several of the others too, as hands at the Rocking C. Some of them she had quizzed about Kingsley's death. She watched as they carried the casket to its final place.

'There's Mary Ellen now,' the woman near Kate whispered again. 'Poor child. Just look at her. She's taking this so very hard.'

The Reverend moved forward and stood at the head of the coffin. He looked toward Mary Ellen and waited, Bible in hand.

Mary Ellen's demeanor, as if she were just holding on by a mere thread, caused the crowd to drift back to let her pass. No one attempted to offer consolation. Kate started toward her, but a tall, dignified man of about thirty reached her first.

He took her arm and guided her forward in a slow, compassionate way. His straight, sandy hair was knotted back with a tie, and he wore a brown Western-style suit that made Kate think of Bill Cody.

'That's her boss,' the old woman whispered, 'that nice Jake Pierson from the museum.'

'I hear he's a bachelor. Wouldn't it be something if . . . ?'

'That's not going to happen. That girl will never marry anyone.'

Jake Pierson, after Mary Ellen was seated, leaned over and gave her a gentlemanly kiss on the cheek, then stepped back into the crowd.

During this interval, Hal Barkley waited impatiently. When his gaze lifted to the grass-covered rise behind them, Kate noted with alarm that his features suddenly changed, becoming hard and angry. 'What's he doing here?'

Swen stood far away from the crowd. He clutched a grey Stetson in his hands, one that matched the colour of his expensive, tailored suit.

Barkley, glaring at Kate, boomed, 'I want you to get him away from us! He's here just to cause trouble.'

'I can't ask him to leave,' Kate replied softly. 'He's not doing anything illegal.'

Kingsley's foreman bristled. 'If you won't, then I will!'

'Leave him alone, Hal,' Jennie said. She rose and laid a restraining hand, one that glittered in the sunlight with diamonds, on Barkley's arm.

Barkley remained a moment, feet planted apart staring toward Swen, then smouldering, he escorted Jennie back to her seat. He took up post on the other side of the casket so he could keep watch on Swen. Kate felt increased apprehension from the fact that whenever she looked up, she faced Hal

Barkley directly.

The Reverend, neat and small of stature, nevertheless had a voice with the ring of William Jennings Bryan. Kate, deep in her own thoughts, didn't listen at first not until his words rose theatrically. 'He should be with us now, reaping the good that he sowed, for Charles Allan Kingsley was a good and faithful man. We cannot gather here as if our beloved friend died peacefully of common causes, for he did not.' He paused, his stillness leaving only the sound of flapping of the tent. 'Whoever committed this wicked act is my enemy, is your enemy, is the enemy of every decent man and woman.'

Kate could not avoid shifting her gaze from the preacher to Hal Barkley. He looked rough with his grizzled beard and stood rigidly straight. Kate had never before in her life seen anyone look so vengeful.

'But, my dear friends, no sin is covered that shall not be revealed.'

Hal Barkley's eyes, dark and hostile, shifted from Swen and clashed with Kate's. To her disconcertion, she felt totally unable to look away.

'I have comfort for you, my friends,' the Reverend said. 'Romans 12:19. I know it's true, because it's written. Here.' He held up the Bible, his words exploding into the stillness, 'Vengeance is mine: I will repay, saith the Lord.'

Kate half-expected the sky overhead to darken, to hear the clack of thunder. She, as well as Hal Barkley, cringed.

'Charles Allan Kingsley, we commend your spirit, not to the grave, for the spirit does not die, but to life eternal!'

After the graveside service ended, people milled around. Mary Ellen, pale and stricken, warding off all expressions of sympathy, started away. Once more she was met and escorted by the kindly museum curator.

The crowd quickly thinned, but Swen remained where he had been throughout the service. Kate, heading towards the squad car, veered off her path to stand beside him.

'Vengeance is mine,' Swen said wryly, staring straight ahead at the casket. 'He should have told that to Kingsley.'

Kate made no reply.

Swen spoke again, his tone low and level. 'I owe him more than I owe any friend I've ever had,' he said.

Side by side they watched the breeze ripple the tent, stir the flag that the Legion had placed beside the coffin. Kate did not look at Swen, but at the grave, thinking of Kingsley, bullet holes in his chest, dead on the floor of his study.

'He was my motivation.' Swen's voice lowered, but remained steady and even. 'The power that drove my success. I spent a lifetime trying to outdo that scoundrel, to be better and bigger than Charles Kingsley.' Swen cast Kate a quick, sideways glance, lined face tight and grim as if in deep grief. 'Strange as it is, I'm going to miss him.'

CHAPTER 4

Kate hung up the phone in Ben's office that had been constantly ringing. Range fires, accidents, domestic violence: everyone wanted access to the Belle County Sheriff. She couldn't keep up, couldn't begin to take care of everything and do justice to the Kingsley case, too.

Kate rose and poured herself a cup of strong coffee. As she took a deep drink, she felt a tight pain in her chest. No wonder Ben was laid up in the hospital. The pressures of the job were transferring themselves from him to her. She rested her forehead against her hand a moment and closed her eyes.

'Tired?' Jeff asked as he entered the room.

'Too much work, not enough time. It's overwhelming.'

'Quit catching the ball,' Jeff suggested with a grin, 'and they'll stop throwing it to you.'

Sometimes she even liked his quips, even

liked him. She smiled. 'Follow your own advice.'

'I might just as well drop the ball for all the credit I get. I can't get over the way you blamed me, thinking I botched the job of contacting Jennie Kingsley. But I swear, if that woman was travelling on the Casper road before or after Kingsley was shot, I would have found her.'

'Not even you can do the impossible,' Kate reminded him. 'If you'll remember, Jennie was driving a borrowed car.' Kate paused. 'I can't help thinking she might have changed more than her car, she may have changed truth to fiction. She may have been right here in Rock Creek at the time Kingsley was shot.'

'Changing truth to fiction, I like that. Did you get that line out of some fancy police-training book?' Jeff flopped down on the chair across from her and propped his booted foot against the desk. 'Face it, the guilty parties are Swen and Garrison. They gunned Kingsley down and put that stone under his head. A gentle soul like Jennie Kingsley would never think of doing something like that.'

'I'm not saying she's either guilty or in-nocent. I'm just stating that she gained more by his death than anyone else. That's why I'm going to drive to Casper and do some checking on her.'

'That's a long way, four hours there, four hours back. Have you ever heard of telephones?'

'If I don't go in person,' Kate replied, 'I'll miss out on all the unspoken testimony.'

'Unspoken testimony — doesn't sound like anything that's going to hold up in court.'

'I would like you to go with me. But if you don't want to, I'll ask Lem.'

'I'll go,' Jeff answered in the same smug way, 'if you'll let me drive.'

Nothing new about that. Jeff always wanted to be in the driver's seat. But today Kate, too weary from the long hours she'd been putting in, didn't mind. As they set out for Casper, Jeff kept up a steady stream of talk.

'For the record, you're wasting your time,' he was declaring. 'Jennie Kingsley's as nice a person as you'd ever meet.'

'Or else you've been taken in, too,' Kate replied. 'She's got looks, she's got charm. Add brains to that combination, and what you've got is power. Power to manipulate blind-sided men like you.'

'So how would I know?' Jeff grinned, casting her a sideways glance. 'No one's ever even tried to victimize me.'

'Wouldn't be worthwhile. Not on a sheriff's salary.'

'What are your plans for today, Kate?'

'I'm looking for a witness who will place Jennie in Casper between eight and midnight and eliminate her as a suspect. I need to clear some other questions up, too. Kingsley had just left Casper Monday afternoon. Why was Jennie in such a hurry to see him again? So much so, that she borrows a car from her friend and gets right on the road?'

When Jeff didn't reply, Kate continued, 'It's a four-hour drive from Casper to Rock Creek. If she left before eight in the evening, she could be at the Rocking C before midnight.'

'Right.'

'That would give her ample time to have shot her new husband and even to have returned to Casper and back.'

'If she's just playing the part of a grieving widow, I want to nominate her for an Oscar.'

Kate paid no attention to his comment. 'Have you noticed how . . . physical she is?'

Jeff grinned again. 'Have I ever.'

'That's not what I mean. I mean Jennie is entirely capable of slamming that pickup into my squad car, ditching it, and striking out to Kingsley's ranch on foot.'

'I won't deny that.'

'Jennie knows she is suspect number one, and she also knows that Kingsley and Swen hated one another. It makes sense that she might try to implicate Swen by using his truck as well as by placing that stone under her husband's head.'

The road had become straight and barren, an endless stretch of slate-coloured land. A herd of white-tailed antelope grazed beyond a snow fence. Kate was now enough of a Wyomingite not to mistake them for deer. Jeff turned at a battered sign.

'Muddy Gap. Halfway there.'

'Bet it's not more than a gas station. It's hard to get used to these miles and miles of nothing.'

Jeff glanced at her, smiling that slow smile of his. 'A good kind of nothing. No crowds, no hassle. Just a lot of wide, open spaces.'

They passed a single oil rig busy at work, looking like a giant, mechanical monster. 'Encroaching civilization,' Jeff said.

The road became steeper, the gentle hills rising to higher peaks as they approached Casper. Before them she saw a sprawling city, small by her standards, even though it was the second largest in Wyoming. 'You call this a city?' she asked. 'You could fit all of Casper into one of Detroit's suburbs.'

'Guess it depends on where you're coming from, Prep,' Jeff replied. 'I grew up on a ranch just outside of Rock Creek. Casper's the big city to me. Even has a mall.' He turned on to a main street. 'What do you say we talk to her neighbours first?'

Kate drew out her notes. 'Turn here. Poison Spider Road.'

'Say, that's a clue,' Jeff teased. 'Where else would a Black Widow live? Just think, this place could be teeming with women who marry men for their money and kill them.'

As Jeff cast her a quick look to judge her reaction, Kate tightened her lips in pretended disgust. 'Ann Lectie, the woman Jennie borrowed the car from, lives on this street, too. The apartment complex where Jennie stays is just a block or two north.'

The building consisted of long, neat rows of houses behind a high-brick fence. 'You take the east side, I'll take the west.'

No one Kate interviewed had seen Jennie at all on Monday. At the end apartment, a woman of about eighty answered the door, eager to talk.

'A little white sports car was parked in Jennie's space,' she said. 'I remember that. I saw it when I went to bed, and it was there when I got up.'

'Do you recall the particular times?'

'At, let's see, nine o'clock, that's when I went to bed, and again at seven, that's when I got up. But the next time I looked out, it was gone, about eight, I'd say.'

'Did you see Jennie? Or were any lights on in her apartment?'

'No, I didn't see her. And I'm afraid I didn't notice whether or not there were any lights on.'

Kate jotted down the woman's name, her apartment and phone number. What she had found out actually meant very little, only that the borrowed car had been in Casper at the time Charles Kingsley was shot.

She shared the information with Jeff. 'What did you find out?'

'Zero. Let's see what Ann Lectie has to say.'

They parked in front of a small, yellow house more run-down than the others in the neighbourhood. An attractive, petite woman with reddish-brown hair answered the door.

'This is my day off. You're lucky to find me home,' she said, inviting them into a room, neat but slightly shabby, as if she had trouble making ends meet.

'Have a seat,' she said, indicating the worn, flowered sofa and matching loveseat.

86

'May I offer you some coffee?'

'No, thanks.' Jeff eased his long form down on the couch and sat, one leg extended. 'We're here to ask a few questions about your friend, Jennie Irwin. Jennie Kingsley now,' he corrected. 'Mrs Kingsley says she borrowed your white Ford Mustang last Monday.'

The mention of Jennie caused a change in her, a nervousness Kate hadn't noticed before.

'Jennie came over to my place about four that afternoon. She said she had been trying to contact Charles, but he didn't answer his cellphone. She told me she was getting worried. Her Buick was in the garage, so she asked to borrow my car. She wanted to head out to Rock Creek. She had a feeling something was wrong. And I guess she was right.'

Ann Lectie directed all of her conversation to Jeff, gazing at him in a wide-eyed sort of way. The woman's full attention caused Kate to look at Jeff, too. It wasn't often that she noticed that he was a very good-looking man.

'Did she go into any details,' Jeff was asking, 'about what she thought might be wrong?'

'Of course she believed he had had an accident on the road.'

'Why do you say "of course"?'

'That's how Jennie lost her first husband. He died in a car crash between here and Buffalo. You know, one where the driver goes to sleep and runs off the road. Charles' health problems increased her anxiety. Jennie kept saying she should never have let him start out alone.'

'But he hadn't been gone all that long.'

'I couldn't blame Jennie for being concerned. She just dearly loved that man. When they weren't together, they were always on the phone.'

'Do you know what time she left for Rock Creek?'

'I thought she was leaving from here, right away, but I guess she didn't. In fact, I know she didn't. I drove the van down to the grocery store about six, and I saw her pass by in my car.'

'Was she alone?' Kate asked.

'As a matter of fact, she wasn't. Some man was in the passenger seat.'

'Did you see him?' Jeff asked. 'Did you recognize him?'

'It gets dark so early now,' Ann said. 'Really all I got was a glimpse of his grey hair. It was kind of a shiny colour.'

Kate thought of Sam Swen, the way his

hair sometimes glistened like silver. She broke in, 'You've been a good friend of Jennie's for some time. Maybe you can tell us more about her. Was she dating someone before she met Mr Kingsley?'

Ann's gaze still held to Jeff. 'Jennie's very sociable. She's always seen friends, although never anything serious. But, wait, there was one man she talked about a lot. He always took her out to dinner whenever he came to Casper.'

'Can you give us a description of him?' Kate asked. 'Do you remember his name?'

'I never met him. He had a funny name. Didn't sound like a first name to me. Breen or something like that.'

'Swen?' Jeff supplied.

'That's it.'

'Then you don't have any idea what time she actually left Casper?' Kate asked.

'I figured she was on her way the minute she left my place. I cautioned her not to drive alone at night. I believe she followed my advice and decided to wait until morning.'

Jeff stood up and handed her one of his cards. 'Thanks for talking to us, Ms Lectie. If you think of anything else of importance, please call me.'

'What's this about? I don't understand

why you're asking me all those questions.'

'We're trying to establish an alibi for her, that's all. Very routine.'

Ann Lectie remained watching from the doorway. Kate glanced back, thinking she looked forlorn and uncertain as if she regretted something she had told them.

This time Kate teased Jeff, 'Ann liked you. I think you could have got a date.'

'Not me. I won't go out with anyone who lives on Poison Spider Road.'

They headed back toward the downtown area, turning on to a tree-filled street nestled in a semi-residential area. Kate spotted the place where Jennie worked first. 'Over there. Talbart's Insurance.'

A distinguished-looking man with an ever-present smile rose from behind a huge desk when they entered. Kate noticed that he had thick, grey hair and wondered if this had been the man Ann had seen in Jennie's car.

He held out his hand to both of them in turn. 'John Talbart.'

'We'd like to have a few words with you about your ex-employee, Jennie Irwin,' Kate said. 'Now Jennie Kingsley.'

'Certainly. I heard about Mr Kingsley's death. Poor Jennie. I must say I was shocked by the news. Robbers everywhere. What's gone wrong with our society anyway?'

He gestured to empty chairs and sank down at his desk beside a large photograph of himself, a plain-looking woman much younger than him, and two small children. He saw Kate looking at the picture, and said proudly, 'That's my wife and family.'

'How long has Jennie Irwin — Kingsley I mean — worked for you?' Jeff asked.

'Going on five years. Jennie's the best help I've ever had. I sometimes think people came in here just to talk to her. I haven't replaced her yet, not that I'll ever be able to. So now I'm my own secretary.'

'When did you see her last?' Kate asked.

'Let me think.' Talbart steepled his fingers together in a thoughtful pose. 'I've been so busy everything runs together. She quit on a Thursday. She had given me notice a week before that, though, but said she would keep on working until I found someone else. I told her, "Don't worry about me. I'll get by".'

'Did you know Mr Kingsley well?'

'Not really. She introduced him to me, that's all.'

'Have you ever heard her mention or have you ever met a man named Sam Swen?' Jeff asked.

'I can't say that I have. But then I meet a lot of people.'

They continued questioning him, but he remained vague and evasive, as if well-schooled by long years of dodging issues. After learning nothing more of help, they rose to leave. At the door, Kate asked, 'Did you see Jennie Kingsley at six o'clock on Monday evening?'

'Monday evening,' Talbart repeated, then said quickly, 'No, as I said, she quit working for me the Thursday before that.'

'I don't trust that one,' Jeff said on the way out of Casper. 'He's too smooth, too guarded. Never answers any question he doesn't want to.' Jeff pulled into a little truck stop. 'Let's get a bite to eat before we head back.'

Jeff selected the kind of café he always chose, homey, with friendly waitresses and plenty of strong black coffee.

An older woman hurried over to their table, saying respectfully, 'What can I get for you two officers?'

Kate's gaze lifted from the booth with its worn, red upholstery and caught the reflection of Jeff and her in the mirror behind the counter: representatives from Belle County sheriff's department in uniform, doing their job. She liked the image, the way people looked at them when they walked into a room. She loved stops like this after a long, hard day, the endless cups of coffee and the companionship of people — she had to admit it — like Jeff, whose concerns were the same as hers.

For a moment she felt a sense of pride. Her parents had been wrong: she loved her job in a way that she never would have loved teaching or any other profession.

'What will you have, Kate?'

She hadn't heard Jeff order, yet she knew he had asked for a hamburger, well done, and fries. 'The same.'

'Jeff, why did you take up police work?' she asked after the waitress had left. 'You've never told me.'

'My dad was a cop. I wanted to follow in his footsteps. He was and is my hero.' Jeff cupped the rim of his coffee mug.

'Bet you didn't stop to think about the gruelling hours and the poor pay.'

Jeff gave one of his slow smiles. 'That's why my last girl broke up with me. Gave me an ultimatum: the job or me.'

'And you took the job?'

'Why not? She was costing me money; the job was paying me.'

'It's not fair for someone to ask you to choose between your work and them.'

'Guess I'll have to marry another cop.' Jeff looked up, his eyes meeting hers, then glanced quickly away.

No, he wouldn't be thinking about her. The two of them would never work out romantically. She could sum Jeff up in a few brief words: always stubborn, often annoying, never boring. But he could probably sum her up in the exact same way. In fact, if they weren't both such obstinate donkeys, always pulling in the opposite direction, they would make a great team.

'You're smiling. What's the joke?'

'You wouldn't want to know,' she replied.

When they reached the outskirts of Rock Creek, Kate asked, 'Has today made you change your mind about anything?'

'No,' Jeff stated. 'I still don't think Jennie had anything to do with Kingsley's murder. Swen knew Kingsley was about to bring a suit against him for rustling cattle so either he or his hired man took him out. Swen's motive was plain and simple: self-protection and revenge.'

'It's all too simple,' Kate replied. 'I just know we're missing something. And Jennie might be a part of it.'

'I think the car in front of her apartment places her in Casper.'

'The car was there, but what about her? And who was the man she was seen with on Monday at six o'clock?'

'Let's just go ask her,' Jeff said. Instead of turning toward the sheriff's office, Jeff swung the patrol car onto the blacktop leading to the Kingsley ranch. The brilliant, glowing yard light made the house look more than ever like some stately Southern mansion. Jennie met them at the door as if she had always owned the Rocking C.

She welcomed them warmly. Her ruffled blonde hair, the jeans and oversized sweatshirt, lettered Casper Rodeo, made her look years younger.

Although she appeared puzzled by their late evening appearance, she seemed more than willing to answer their questions.

'I followed Ann's advice,' Jennie told them. 'I stayed in Rock Creek until about eight the next morning, then when I still couldn't reach Charles, I headed right out.'

Kate studied her as she spoke, trying to measure the effects of her words. 'Ann said she saw you about six Monday evening and that some man was in the car with you.'

A somewhat perplexed frown cut between Jennie's eyes, as if this turn of events had not been anticipated. 'That would be my boss, John Talbart,' she told them. 'I remembered some unfinished business and thought I should discuss it with him before I left town.'

'Trouble is,' Jeff returned, 'Mr Talbart claims he wasn't in your car that evening.'

Jennie flashed a quick, disarming smile. 'He would say that. John has a very jealous wife. He gives her no reason at all to doubt him, but he would never admit to seeing any woman after office hours. What does it matter anyway?'

'We are trying to help you establish an alibi.'

'Knowing where I was at six o'clock wouldn't be much help,' Jennie said, 'not when my husband wasn't killed until midnight. What do you really want to know?'

Kate didn't hesitate. 'Were you seeing someone besides Charles Kingsley?'

'Definitely not.'

Jeff looked relieved. 'We're very sorry we bothered you so late,' he said.

Jennie walked with them to the entrance, waving as they pulled away. Jennie remained motionless, framed in the brilliant glow of light, and for a moment Kate had the strange illusion that Sam Swen, Charles Kingsley's arch-enemy, was standing in the doorway beside her.

CHAPTER 5

Saturday arrived, Kate's day off. In fact, her turn had come to have the entire weekend free. Glad to be just plain Kate Jepp again, she slipped into jeans and a comfortable pullover sweater. Despite the fact that she was on her own time, she couldn't drive the Kingsley case from her mind or that curious invitation to Tom Horn's hanging on the wall behind the dead man's desk. It kept arising, as if intricately connected to the crime, despite the fact that, ironically, it had not been stolen.

The image of that handwritten letter, signed by the sheriff of Laramie County in 1903, prompted Kate to stop at the local museum to find out all she could about this relic from Wyoming's bloody past.

Even though the museum's curator, Jake Pierson, didn't recognize her, Kate had noticed him at the funeral, offering kind consolation to Mary Ellen. He strode forward, his greeting friendly: 'Welcome to the Belle County Museum.'

Once more, his longish tied-back hair and the fringed buckskin jacket he wore put her in mind of Bill Cody.

'I'm interested,' she said, 'in the history of Tom Horn.'

'That makes us two of a kind, then,' he replied. The affable smile that remained on his lips suggested a person of vast interests, one who would have no trouble identifying with people, past or present.

Kate followed him towards a huge portrait of a man who looked bold and swaggering — larger than life — even on canvas. Pierson stared up at the painting, empathy reflecting in his pale, intelligent eyes.

'Tom Horn started out as an army scout,' he said. 'Brave too, rode alone into an Indian camp and negotiated Geronimo's surrender. After that, he spent time as a Pinkerton detective, chasing bank and train robbers.' The curator's alert eyes shifted to Kate. 'Unfortunately, he worked both inside and outside the law. His name should "live in infamy" as President Roosevelt would have said, as a fierce gunman and hired killer.'

Kate studied Tom Horn's handsome face; he didn't look like any cold-blooded murderer. 'Men like him are hard to figure out, aren't they? Maybe that's why today we're still fascinated by his story.'

'He's a legend, all right,' the curator agreed with great respect, 'a symbol of the Old West, its code of honor and its cruel justice. Even today some find him admirable, his deeds justified.'

Tom Horn's strong air of mystery, the square set of his shoulders, and the tilt of his head made Kate think of men like Sam Swen and Ty Garrison. Independence, individuality, fearlessness: heroes and those who lived outside the law often possessed the same qualities.

'I've always been drawn to outlaws,' Jake Pierson mused, his gaze returning to the painting.

'Me too, but not from a historical perspective.'

He turned toward her, looking at her closely. As he did, recognition glinted in his eyes. 'I knew you looked familiar. I saw you at Kingsley's funeral, didn't I? Just failed to recognize you out of uniform. When you came in, I took you to be a student looking for information for a paper.'

'I do need information.'

'About Tom Horn?' Pale eyes became impish as he quipped, 'Is he a suspect?'

'In a way. What else can you tell me about him?'

Jake Pierson hesitated a moment and she sensed his attitude toward her had undergone a subtle change. 'Sam Swen's the local expert on Tom Horn, not me.'

Taken by surprise at his remark, she didn't pursue it, only said, 'You're doing fine.'

'I've written several articles about the man myself,' Pierson went on, a bit reluctantly now. 'Around 1892 Horn began working for the Wyoming Cattle Grower's Association. He had been hired as a horse breeder, but his real job was to track down rustlers. One day, Horn lay in wait for a man named Kels P. Nickell, a rival rancher who had been targeted for death.' Pierson's voice lowered slightly. 'By mistake, he ended up shooting Nickell's fourteen-year-old son. The boy was tall for his age and had taken out his father's wagon.'

'A tragic error.'

'That's why Tom Horn was hanged. But many people today still swear by him.'

'Not very brave hiding in the bushes and taking pot-shots at unarmed men,' Kate remarked.

'Depends which side you're on. Horn classified cattle rustlers with wolves and coyotes and considered himself a benefactor for stamping them out. To people like Sam Swen, that makes him a genuine hero.'

'Why did he place under the heads of his victims that . . . stone of vengeance?'

'I see you've been talking to Swen,' Jake Pierson replied with a laugh. 'Swen's the one who coined that phrase, you know. He's the man who began calling Tom Horn's trademark the "Stone of Vengeance".'

Kate had without thinking used the same term herself. In the stillness she recalled how Swen had told her that Tom Horn was only doing the law's job, and the memory caused a chill to go through her.

'Something wrong?' Pierson asked.

'No. I was just wondering how they caught him.'

Pierson gave another of his short laughs. 'They wouldn't have, if Horn hadn't got drunk one night and started boasting. When they put him in jail he broke out, but he didn't get far on foot. Innocent or guilty, he spent his last days writing his memoirs and weaving the rope they used to hang him.'

'In Charles Kingsley's study there's an invitation to Tom Horn's hanging.'

Jake paused in a moment of sadness. 'Too bad about Charles. I hope they find the person who shot him.'

'We're trying.'

'Charles Kingsley and Swen were sworn enemies, did you know that?' he asked. 'I only met Charles once, but he seemed like a really nice fellow. Of course, I'm more acquainted with Mary Ellen. She volunteers here, you know.' In a kindly manner he said, 'Poor Mary Ellen. She seems so lost and lonely sometimes. Working here does her the world of good.'

'Have you been in Rock Creek long, Mr Pierson?'

'No. I just came to town about five months ago. I was a friend of the recent curator's so when he retired, I took over his job.'

'I suppose you've seen Mr Kingsley's Western artifacts?'

'Mary Ellen insisted on showing them to me once. Quite a collection.'

'I'm thinking that the killer might have broken into the Kingsley ranch intending to steal these items. A robbery in progress, that Kingsley interrupted. Do you have any idea what that invitation to Tom Horn's hanging would be worth?'

The curator hesitated. 'That little bit of paper is probably the most valuable item in Charles' collection.'

'How much money are we talking about?'

'That depends,' Jake Pierson replied. 'I'd say under certain circumstances, it could bring between fifty to eighty thousand.'

Kate drew in her breath. 'That much?'

'Only a handful of those invitations still exist and,' he added after another dry little chuckle, 'of course, there won't be any more.'

'I wouldn't think everyone would want an invitation to a hanging decorating their parlour wall.'

'You'd be surprised,' Jake Pierson returned. 'Letters and documents from well-known people are highly desirable. Any serious collector of Western memorabilia would love to get their hands on that little section of history. Why, I'd like to own it myself.'

Jake Pierson didn't need to have added that — the fact shone clearly in his eyes.

'For the museum collection, of course,' he added quickly, as if reading her thoughts. 'I asked Mrs Kingsley if she'd consider selling or even donating some items to the museum, but she turned me down flat. Can't really blame her.'

'So you know Jennie Irwin? Jennie Kingsley now,' Kate corrected.

'I met her at the funeral and once after it to talk about purchasing the collection.'

He hadn't wasted much time, Kate thought.

'But, back to what you were saying, I

don't think anyone would break in to steal that invitation. Even though it is a great prize, no buyer would touch it. It would lead a trail right to his door.'

Kate must not have looked convinced.

'Because of the Kingsley name on it,' Pierson went on, 'a thief wouldn't dare try to sell it.'

'Not unless he had a ready buyer,' Kate said, 'one willing to look the other way, to purchase on a "don't ask, don't tell" basis.' Her thoughts turned to Sam Swen and his interest in Tom Horn. What would he pay to get his hands on an item related to a historical figure he admired, one that belonged to his arch-enemy, Charles Kingsley? 'Or, maybe whoever broke in didn't intend to sell it.'

'Could be. We'll probably never know.'

Kate began to walk towards the door, and Jake Pierson followed. Halfway across the room a cattle painting caught her eye. 'Beautiful Herefords,' she observed.

Jake Pierson laughed. 'Don't say that too loudly around here.'

'Why not?'

'There's quite a story behind that painting. The original by Dutch painter Paul Potter once hung on the walls of the exclusive Cheyenne Club. You've probably heard of that place.'

'Yes.'

Jake Pierson's love of history animated his words as he said, 'Members of the powerful Wyoming Stock Grower's Association used to gather there for a taste of culture and companionship. The painting became notorious around 1895 when a wealthy rancher by the name of John Coble, Tom Horn's boss, was suspended from the club for shooting holes in the leg of one of the painted bulls.'

'Why did he do that?'

The smile remained on the curator's face. 'He admitted he had been drinking. But he had few regrets about the shooting. You see, Coble was a bit of a cattle snob. In his own words, the painting was "a travesty on purebred stock".'

'How can you tell the difference?'

'To an untrained eye, it might be difficult.'

Kate was beginning to like his laugh, quick and appreciative.

'But the critters in this picture are not from the pure Hereford line that originated in Herefordshire, England. A cattleman can spot them on sight, just as a dog breeder can tell an Irish setter from a mutt. Purebreds have white faces and reddish-brown bodies. The poor creatures in this painting are as spotted as Dalmatians. They've obviously been crossed with another breed, which makes them the mutts of the cattle world, cattle that ranchers like Coble would never condescend to raise.' He paused significantly. 'There's big money in the purebred Herefords.'

'You seem to know as much about ranching as you do about history.'

'I grew up on a ranch. In Montana.'

That explained the rough, work-hardened hands with their big, bony knuckles.

'That kind of snobbery exists today the same way it did years ago. Except now there's fewer and fewer small ranchers. In Montana big ruthless cattle barons have already gobbled up most of them.' Grimness crept into his voice. 'My daddy went broke and moved to Helena, but he never recovered.' Pierson stood for a moment looking at the picture. 'From what I hear, things haven't changed much around here either. People like Swen and Kingsley still live that way, knocking over anyone who gets in their way.'

'That always seems the case when there's a lot at stake. How much would one of these animals be worth?'

Jake Pierson shrugged. 'The price varies, of course, but I suppose a good Hereford bull could run a couple of thousand. Or even more.'

That meant both Sam Swen and Charles Kingsley had a gold mine roaming around in their pastures, money ripe for the taking, open to anyone who had the means and opportunity to steal and transport stolen cattle.

Although Kate had visited the museum for an entirely different reason, her thoughts had come full circle. Kingsley's murder might centre on cattle rustling after all. Although that seemed the plausible answer, Kate still found herself clinging to the idea that the killer's motivation went much deeper than what was seen on the surface. The Tom Horn hanging and the cattle rustling: if only she could find a link between the two.

'Thank you for your time, Mr Pierson. You've been very helpful.'

'Helping people understand history, that's my job and my joy.'

Kate left the museum thinking that the murder of Charles Kingsley had to have been committed by someone who knew all about the legend of Tom Horn and the feud between Sam Swen and Charles Kingsley. All the evidence seemed to point directly — almost too directly — to Sam Swen. Perhaps, just as he had claimed, he was being cleverly set up to take the blame. Either way, someone had purposefully placed that stone beneath Kingsley's head, that ominous 'Stone of Vengeance'.

Feeling a little weary, in need of a quiet place to be alone and think, Kate cut across the street to the Tumbleweed Café. Everything here was named after something Western: the Cowboy Motel, the Lazy Z Tavern, the Outlaw gas station on the corner. After her move from Auburn Hills, Michigan, it had taken time for Kate to adjust to life in a small Wyoming town. The laid-back atmosphere, the single main street, the buildings with their Old West facades, was a far cry from the bustling city and the suburban neighbourhood where her parents and younger sister still lived. Here, everyone knew everyone else's business.

But Kate had also discovered advantages: little need to lock doors at night, no long lines at the single supermarket, and finding a parking space on main street never posed a problem. Moreover, the local restaurant served good, home-cooked food.

Kate's job kept her so busy that often she simply grabbed a sandwich, so most weekends she headed for the Tumbleweed and ordered their Ranch Hand Special, which consisted today of chicken fried steak.

When her meal came, she began to eat hungrily.

'Now there's what I like to see,' a deep voice spoke up, 'a girl with a hearty appetite.'

Ty Garrison, free of the air of guarded aloofness that Kate had noted at Swen's ranch, was walking towards her, his lean, broad-shouldered form seeming to swagger in the hazy sunlight that streamed from the window. His hair looked thick, streaked with gold, much lighter than she recalled, but his eyes seemed darker, more intense.

He didn't ask permission to join her, just slipped into the opposite side of the booth. He called to the waitress to bring him the special and a strong cup of coffee.

Kate liked the change in him. The bruise along the line of his jaw had faded and warmth lit his eyes. Today he seemed to really see her, Kate the person, not Kate the sheriff.

Their conversation was marked with laughs and banter until Kate asked, 'How did you end up working for Swen?'

At her question he grew grave and thoughtful. 'Just got back to Rock Creek. I had worked for him once before in a roundup when I was little more than a kid.' Ty slanted her a glance, then went on hesitantly, as if this were something about which he seldom spoke. 'Swen gave me a job to do and I let him down. Got drunk and ended up in jail, wound up costing Swen money. I thought he'd fire me. I came around to apologize, but he only told me, "You don't have to answer to me, you have to answer to yourself".'

'And that's what you do now?' Kate returned lightly, wishing she had not brought up this serious subject.

'I looked up to Swen, mostly because he's the only one who ever gave me a second chance. Not to mention good advice.' Ty's smile appeared again. 'Of course, most of it I didn't follow. Couldn't really, because trouble seems to track me around. I should have stayed with him then instead of striking out on my own. Made a big mess of those next years.'

'What did you do?'

Acting as if he wanted to avoid any answer, he said evasively, 'Just wandered around, mostly.'

'In Wyoming?'

'For the most part. I just went back to drifting. Ended up working on a ranch over in Coal County. I was having problems with my boss there, we just didn't see eye to eye. So when I ran across Swen one day in Casper, and he said he needed me, that he was having a lot of trouble at the ranch, I jumped at his offer of a steady job. So here I am. But now, Kate, tell me all about yourself.'

'Not much to tell,' she replied. 'I was born in Detroit. My parents were both opposed to my taking up police work. Mum wanted me to go into teaching; that's what my sister Allison plans to do.'

'They don't like the danger involved in your job. Can't blame them for that.'

'I graduated from the Michigan Police Academy, where I got my degree in Criminal Justice. The boys here will never let me live it down.'

His clear, brown eyes met hers admiringly. 'I think we're a lot alike, not afraid to take a chance and follow our hearts. I needed a job where I could be free, not confined behind a desk all day.' He watched her carefully.

'I went into law enforcement because I like to see wrongs righted.'

'So do I,' Ty replied, 'in my own way.'

His words made her think of Tom Horn's slant on justice. The thought caused the closeness between them to take distance. 'Are you certain there's no truth in the lawsuit Kingsley intended to bring against Swen?'

'Swen, a cattle thief?' Ty shook his head. 'At first I thought Kingsley had got that foreman of his, Hal Barkley, to set this all up simply to cause trouble for Swen. But now I'm not so sure.'

'Why?'

Ty's eyes, like his hair, seeming an indefinite colour, now glinted with flecks of yellow light. 'Like I told you the other day, we may be dealing with a professional ring of thieves hitting both ranches. Kingsley must have found some evidence out in the vast canyon between our lands that he misinterpreted and linked with Swen.'

The bright sheen disappeared from his eyes and left them dark and moody. 'Anyway, it's not over yet. Whatever's going on, I intend to settle it.'

Once again the Tom Horn image merged with Ty's. 'Not a very wise idea,' Kate said, 'to take the law into your own hands.'

He made no reply.

'That's what Tom Horn did.' In the stillness Kate thought of Charles Kingsley lying dead in his study, then of Tom Horn, a hired gun who had been willing to go to any lengths to protect his boss.

'Don't worry. I'm not like that.'

Suddenly, as if to bridge the great empty space between them, Ty reached across the table and caught her hand. She felt the warm, strong pressure of his grasp and wished that the two of them had met under different circumstances.

'You're the first girl I've seen who makes me think of flowers. May I send you some? A dozen red roses.'

'I couldn't accept any gifts from you.' Kate smiled to take the edge from her words. 'Besides, I'm a wild flower person.'

'Then I have a great idea. Let's go out and view the autumn flowers. Since you're not working today, why don't you head out to the ranch this afternoon? I'll put together a picnic. We'll saddle up the horses and ride out into the canyon land. It's beautiful there.'

Just at that moment, she saw Jeff walk by the café, slow his steps and look in. His jaw tightened as his gaze fastened on her and Ty, then he moved quickly away. Kate wondered how long it would take Jeff to get word to Ben Addison that she was having dinner with a prime suspect in the Kingsley case.

Kate removed her hand from his. 'Ty, I'd like to, but I can't.'

Kate continued looking at the vacant

window where moments ago Jeff had stood watching. She wished she wasn't the sheriff and that Ty wasn't a major suspect in her investigation. But that was fact and that fact prevented her from following her heart.

Back at the office, Kate kept thinking about the statements both the owners of the Rocking C and the Double S had made concerning stolen stock. Both ranches claimed to be the target of cattle thefts which, according to Ty, were still occurring. That meant that the rustlers, able to make such bold strikes, possessed some sure and easy method of turning the stock into quick cash.

On the computer Kate pulled up a listing of Wyoming's livestock auctions. The closest one, as well as the largest, was Pauley's Auction Barn in Downing. She jotted this address down, as well as several others.

Feeling hostile eyes on her, Kate glanced up to see Jeff's tall solid form blocking the doorway to her office. The way his broad jaw thrust forward added an unusual look of aggression to his generally laid-back appearance. As did his stance, rigidly straight, hands at his sides as if ready for some dark-alley shoot-out.

'Just what on earth do you think you're doing?'

Kate shrugged. 'Investigating.'

'Is that why you were just holding hands with Ty Garrison? Is that the way you investigate?'

When Kate made no reply, Jeff's voice grew louder. 'You're not playing test scores at your highfaluting little college now. The driver of that truck meant to harm you. You'd better start putting two and two together, young lady. You had just left Swen's ranch. No one but them knew you were anywhere in the area. Swen wanted to stop your prying, so he sent Garrison after you. So tell me, what do you mean getting all chummy with Ty Garrison, of all people?'

Kate thought she saw a spark of something — was it jealousy — in his eyes. She looked at him with surprise. Could Jeff harbour a special interest in her and was that the source of his sometimes merciless teasing? No, she had pegged that correctly from the beginning when she had chalked his attitude down to petty professional envy, envy that was surfacing again now.

Jeff stepped closer to her, hands on his hips. 'Even though you seem to think you're invisible, the whole town saw you with him.'

'I needed information,' Kate said. 'Ty believes we may be dealing with professional cattle rustlers who are hitting both ranches.'

'Of course, he'd say that,' Jeff replied caustically, 'to divert suspicion away from himself.'

Kate knew that Jeff wasn't going to listen. His mind was dead set against the Double S. He had already pegged Ty and Swen as co-conspirators. But Kate wasn't that hasty to make a judgment. Kingsley's being able to identify the cattle rustlers could very well have been the cause of his murder. But if someone were rustling cattle from both ranches, and the thefts hadn't stopped with Kingsley's death, Swen and Ty might also be in danger.

'I want you to back off, Kate,' Jeff said belligerently. 'I'll handle the Double S myself.'

'I can't do that. My investigation. . . .'

'Not just yours, Kate,' he cut her off. 'Mine, too.'

For a short time, when he had accompanied her to Casper, Jeff and Kate had been able to work on the case together harmoniously. Now, Jeff seemed once more her opposition. All along she had chalked up his attitude to petty rivalry and was able to overlook it, now she felt threatened. If she couldn't pacify him, trouble would erupt, trouble she might not be able to handle.

'What do you think I should be doing?'

'Certainly not dating Ty Garrison.'

'Ty invited himself to my table. What was I supposed to do, grab my plate and run away? It certainly wasn't a date.'

'Tell that to Ben, not to me. I've seen the way Garrison looks at you.' Jeff swung around, as if feeling the same flare of anger that was sweeping through her. 'If you want my opinion, I think you should take yourself off this case!'

It took some time after Jeff had stormed out for Kate to get back to the task at hand. She finished her research on the computer and concluded that Pauley's Auction Barn would be her best bet at finding out more about both Swen and Charles Kingsley's operations.

CHAPTER 6

As Kate approached Pauley's Auction Barn, the strong scent of hay and cattle made her think of county fairs, of ribbons pinned on prize-winning livestock. The parking lot was crammed with pickups and four-wheel drives, many hitched with stock trailers. Kate circled the driveway and found a place to park near the stalls and corrals that spanned the area beyond the main building.

Kate remained in the Landcruiser watching the milling cattle and the cowboys in worn boots and Stetsons who were speculating over prices and values. Taking on the same appraising manner, Kate left her vehicle and walked along the fence examining the consigned livestock.

In no time she spotted a brand she recognized, the Rocking C of the Kingsley ranch. The rocking part, probably to make it different from other ranches by that name, was not attached to the C, but set several inches beneath it, forming a bow that looked like the mouth of a happy face. After examining the Kingsley cattle, she moved on.

Further down the line, she located the Double S brand. The overflowing corral pointed to the fact that Sam Swen was the auction's biggest consigner. Nothing surprising about that; Pauley's was the closest cattle auction to Swen's ranch, naturally he would do most of his selling here.

Kate leaned over the fence to take a closer look. Was it her imagination, or did some of the brands look rough and uneven? Swen's brand, consisting of two large S's so close together that one was almost a shadow of the other, stood out much thicker and bolder than Kingsley's imprint of the Rocking C. Kate took out a pad and pen and easily transformed a Rocking C into one of Swen's large S's, then she added another close beside it.

Yet she couldn't forget that Swen had complained of missing cattle, too. She drew a double S this time, but no matter what she did, the connection between the C and the rocking bar could not be hidden. It would be impossible to change an S into a Rocking C or at least very difficult. She imagined with some careful work it could be accomplished, but probably not without leaving behind some tell-tale signs of brand tampering. The fact that it would be so much easier for Swen to alter Kingsley's brand to his own than vice versa gave more credibility to the fact that Swen had been stealing from Kingsley and not the other way around.

Still it didn't seem likely that Swen would risk selling Kingsley's cattle at the same auction where the Rocking C did their trading. Unless Swen had got too bold, too sure of himself and Kingsley had, at this very auction, found proof that Swen was selling his cattle. If so, then Kingsley's evidence for his lawsuit must have centred around alteration of his brand or some discrepancy in sales records held by the company.

Kate, while she was here, would talk to the proprietor of Pauley's Auction Barn. From Swen's record of sales over the past few years, she might be able to detect suspicious rises in the number of cattle he had been selling; rises that might coincide with the dates on Kingsley's missing stock.

Feeling suddenly uneasy, Kate glanced around to see a skinny man, hands in the pockets of his jeans jacket, watching her. He turned away so swiftly she couldn't see his face, only strands of stringy pale yellow hair poking from beneath the hat that slouched over his eyes.

She started towards the main building, drawing to an uncertain halt beside a sign that read, 'Auction 2 p.m. Today'. She looked behind again, but the man who had been watching her must have ducked into one of the adjoining buildings. She passed through the double doors into an arena surrounded with bleachers, alive with loud conversation and movement, with the excitement of an auction.

Kate followed a circular side corridor, which dead-ended into an open door marked 'OFFICE'. She stepped into a waiting room cluttered with worn books and piles of cattle-and-feed magazines

'What can I do you for?' a voice called out over the waist-high partition. As he spoke he rose, leaning his arms on the frame that separated them and beaming an appreciative smile. 'Auction starts in twenty minutes. Too late to consign today.'

'I'm not here to sell cattle.'

The smile grew wider, showing a spread of yellowed teeth. He sported a scraggly brown Willy Nelson style beard and a red baseball cap with the name Pauley's Auction Barn emblazoned across the top. 'Then what can I do for you, little lady?'

'I need to talk to the manager.'

'That would be me. Hank Pauley. In the flesh.'

'I'm Kate Jepp from the sheriff's department.'

Pauley's smile quickly faded. A wad of Skoal hit the nearby waste can, thudding as it struck the metal edge. 'Where's your uniform? Where's your badge? How do I know you're who you say you are?' he asked suspiciously.

Kate handed him ID marked 'Belle County Sheriff's Department, Kate Jepp, Deputy'.

He studied it in a manner more belligerent now than suspicious, then returned it. 'So what do you want?'

'I need to take a look at the sales records of both Charles Kingsley and Sam Swen.'

'Why?'

'You've heard, haven't you, about Mr Kingsley's death? This is a routine part of our investigation.'

'Routine, is it? Why's that?'

'Did Mr Kingsley ever talk to you about his cattle being rustled?'

She waited for his answer. No matter what he claimed, Kate had already begun to question his honesty.

'He never mentioned it to me,' Pauley returned curtly.

'I'd like to start with Swen's bills of sales for the last two years.'

This request brought a dark, sullen look to his eyes, a look of resistance. 'All sales made through my auction house are confidential.'

'Then it looks as if I'll have to return with a court order.'

'You just do that,' Pauley snapped. 'I don't like being bullied, you need to understand that. And I'm not showing you anything until I see something official.'

Pauley had won that round, and probably would the next one too. If some dirty dealing were going on, he'd use the time it would take her to get a warrant to make a new set of records, ones that would show no abnormalities. 'Have you seen any evidence of tampering, of brand alteration in the cattle?'

'Lady, I'm a square-shooter. If I don't like the looks of the brand, I call Ben.'

'To my knowledge you've never done that.'

She should have stifled that comeback. Kate's words brought an ugly, downward twist to his lips, a forewarning that he would say no more on the subject.

They stared at one another. Out in the arena a booming voice sounded over the loudspeaker. 'The sale starts in ten minutes.

Be sure folks to get a number. You'll want to be ready to bid. As you know, Pauley offers the best deals ever to go over the block.'

'As you can see,' Pauley said, 'I have a business to run. And I can't be letting you keep me from it.'

Kate couldn't force him to cooperate. All she could do was accept his dismissal and leave. She did so quickly, almost running squarely into the same man who had been watching her earlier. He stepped away from where he had been lurking close to the open doorway listening to their every word. Hurriedly, he pulled the brim of his hat lower over his face and ducked past her into the office. But not before she glimpsed his face, his long, angular features, his pasty skin.

Frightening, she thought. She increased the pace of her steps, glad to join the crowd of people waiting for the sale to begin.

Not until she was safe in her Landcruiser heading out of town did she begin to breathe easier. Even though she hadn't found any clear-cut evidence, she had felt undercurrents of something amiss, which alerted her that she was on the right trail.

At the outskirts of the small town of Downing, she turned on to a deserted road that offered a shortcut back to Rock Creek. Soon, hers was the only vehicle around. No movement, only miles of hills and sagebrush and a narrow asphalt trail filled with pits and ruts. Kate still wasn't used to driving thirty or more miles without seeing so much as a town or even a gas station. She wondered if she would ever quite get used to the total isolation of the Wyoming countryside.

Kate had driven for a number of miles before she noticed the Landcruiser was becoming very difficult to steer. Then a fierce wobbling started at the back wheel. Before she could pull over to stop, the vehicle veered crazily to the right. A loud thud sounded. She frantically gripped the wheel, but no longer had any control. Despite her attempts to keep it on the road, the Landcruiser careened to the side and plummeted over a steep embankment. She braced herself, expecting the heavy vehicle to roll, instead it came to a jolting stop midway down the slope.

Images flashed before her eyes, of night and the black truck that had crashed into her squad car. Eyes tightly closed, she slumped over the wheel, trying to catch her breath, trying to stop trembling. She could have been badly injured. As it was, she was only shaken and stranded.

The Landcruiser sat at an uneven tilt.

With some effort Kate pulled open the door and climbed out to appraise the damage. She had supposed she had blown a tyre, but to her amazement the one on the back passenger side had pulled completely loose from the axle.

She stood, chilled by the sweeping wind. What would cause this to happen? As if in answer, the thin cruel features of the yellow-haired cowboy flashed before her. He had definitely been watching, eavesdropping on her conversation with Pauley. With the sale beginning, he could have returned to the fast-emptying parking lot and sabotaged her vehicle.

But it was just as likely that some station attendant had forgotten to tighten the lug bolts when she had taken the vehicle in for new tyres a few days ago. Right now, that was what she preferred to believe.

Kate shivered and reached into the front seat for her jacket, fumbling in the pocket for her cellphone. She suddenly had a visual image of it lying where she had left it on the kitchen table. That was the trouble with cellphones; she never had one handy when it was really needed.

Kate slipped on her jacket. She located the tyre where it had come to a smashing stop in the rocky gully below. The accident had caused a split along the rim, but she had a spare that should get her home.

Another gust of wind caused a chill to rush over her, even through the heavy jacket. All alone, on a seldom used road, she couldn't help feeling vulnerable. Once more, the disturbing thought slipped into her mind that the cowboy might have set a trap, intending to waylay her.

The thought brought with it fear and increased activity. She rolled the ruined tyre up to the Landcruiser where she took out the spare and the jack. She finally got the jack to hold against the uneven ground but knew, even as she did, that the task before her was hopeless. The way the heavy vehicle was positioned so askew, she would never be able to lift the back high enough to replace the tyre. Because of the precarious way the Landcruiser swayed to the side, steel from the tyreless frame embedded into earth, she wouldn't even attempt to drive it back up to the road.

Breathing hard, Kate abandoned her efforts and made her way up the slope. She stood, shivering as she looked up and down the road for the signs of a ranch, seeing only the dead stillness of endless grassland.

She waited, feeling helpless, desperately hoping that some motorist would happen along. Kate had no sooner made the wish, than she heard the sound of a distant motor.

Had it been approaching from the direction of the auction barn, she would have been afraid, but this vehicle was coming from Rock Creek, so whoever was behind the wheel could not have been following her.

A polished Dodge truck with a showy, silver Double S ornament on the hood pulled to a stop. Sam Swen, taking his time, stepped out. He remained motionless for a while, the wind tugging at his tweed jacket and ruffling through his silver hair. Kate's heart sank. He was last person she wanted to see now. His sudden appearance couldn't spring from pure coincidence.

Swen's eyes, grey and narrowed, flitted toward the Landcruiser. 'Looks as if you could use some help. Did you have a blowout?'

'The tyre just came off — worked itself loose.'

'Strange,' he said, moving closer to appraise the situation. 'I'll have to get your Landcruiser out of that ditch before I can change the tyre. I've got a chain in my toolbox, so I'll just pull it up to level ground.'

He started to say something else but was stopped by the ringing of his cellphone. He took it from his pocket, saying, 'Swen.' He listened for a while, then spoke again, his voice lowering. 'I'm going to be a little late.' The response of the person on the other end of the line caused him to frown, to step away from Kate, as if to ensure privacy.

Dread filled Kate. She couldn't make out what Swen was saying, but as sure as if she had heard his every word, she knew the call concerned her. When he hung up she said, 'I appreciate your help. If you can get the car levelled so my jack will work, I can do the rest. No use your missing an appointment.'

'Call me old-fashioned,' Swen said, 'but I'd never leave a lady stranded on the road. Now, you just step back, and I'll have you up and running in no time.'

Effortlessly, working with agile motions like a young man, Swen expertly guided the vehicle up to the road. He got out and going around to the aluminum toolbox said, 'Got a hydraulic jack that will work much better than what you have.'

'I could never have moved the vehicle without help,' she told him, and added, even though she didn't feel that her words contained any truth. 'I'm so lucky you came along.'

'This old road doesn't get much traffic,'

he responded.

'Where were you headed?' she asked.

'I was just on my way to Pauley's Auction Barn. Like to watch my stock sell. Keep up on the prices firsthand.'

'I just came from there myself.'

'You don't say.' He cast her an amused glance. 'I hope you don't plan on getting into the cattle business. I don't need the competition.'

'I went there as part of my investigation,' she replied. As she spoke the words, she became more aware than ever that they were all alone out here, not another person in sight. She thought again of the peroxide-haired cowboy, who could be on Sam Swen's payroll.

Swen's look darkened. 'I was just talking to Pauley on the cellphone. He said the law had just been out there asking questions about his operation. Appears you upset him.'

In silence Kate watched as he worked the jack.

'Bolts didn't break, at least that's good,' he said, positioning the spare tyre in place. 'Now all we need are lug nuts. We'll just borrow one from each of the other tyres. That'll get you home, but make sure you remember to replace them as soon as you get back into town. Hand me that tyre iron.'

Swen moved over to the driver's side and knelt by the tyre there. When he looked up at her, a frown cut between his eyes, which again had narrowed and darkened. 'Did you talk to anyone at the auction besides Pauley?'

'Why do you ask that?'

'Because from the looks of this, I'd say you made yourself an enemy.'

'What do you mean?'

'I mean the lug nuts on this side are loose, too. This wasn't any accident. Someone set you up.'

Swen rose slowly, features tight and hard, tyre iron still in hand. A perfect weapon, she thought, capable of crushing someone's skull. Kate took an uneasy step backwards. For a moment, she found herself afraid of this powerful man who had stopped, supposedly to help her.

'It's a lonely road between Downing and Rock Creek,' Swen said. 'Not a lot of traffic. I'd say whoever did this might have wanted to catch you stranded out here alone.'

'I haven't seen anyone but you since I left town.'

Swen gazed down the road that would lead to Pauley's Auction. 'Trouble is, you don't see people like that. But they see you. Anyway, I must have scared them off.'

He gathered the chain and the jack and placed it back in his truck before he spoke again. 'Or maybe whoever did this just wanted to cause an accident, teach you a little lesson.'

A cold chill crept down Kate's spine that had nothing to do with the strong wind that buffeted her jacket. Either way, someone had sabotaged her Landcruiser as a warning for her to stay away from Pauley's, to stop her investigation of the cattle rustling.

'I'd say this was some kind of a friendly warning,' Swen said. Swen remained ever the gentleman, but she sensed in his manner what could be a thinly veiled threat. 'Maybe your last one.'

CHAPTER 7

Kate stood gazing from the sheriff's office out into the street. Bright sunlight glinted against the buildings, making them look old and timeworn. A pleasant day, filled with the brilliant colours and the clear, brisk air of autumn; once more she felt a pang of regret that she had turned down the date with Ty yesterday. For a moment she became caught up with images of Ty, riding a tall white Arabian horse, wind sweeping through his hair.

Wearily she turned from the window. Everything concerning this crime remained a jumble. Her instincts, which she had always relied on so completely, ran counter to the facts.

She crossed Ben's office and entered the evidence room. For a long time she sat at the wooden table studying the single earring found in Swen's truck, one she still believed belonged to either Mary Ellen or

Jennie. Although she had been keeping close watch, neither woman had mentioned losing an earring or had worn a matching bracelet or necklace. Regardless, feeling this might be some vital clue, Kate set the earring aside.

She concentrated on sifting through the contents of the glove compartment of the truck. She studied the registration, the co-op and feed stores invoices, then carefully unfolded the single, remaining item: a tattered map of Belle County.

Three small x's spaced far apart had been marked in pen on the map. She frowned in concentration. Two were on Kingsley's land, one on Swen's. This alone, seemed to possess some sinister significance.

In addition three phone numbers had been scribbled on the yellowed margin. The first two were written in blue ink, the last in black. Kate lost no time running a check on the numbers. One belonged to Pratt's Insurance Company, one to a rancher from Laramie and — bingo — the final one from Casper, was listed under the name of Jennie Irwin.

Kate stuffed the map into her canvas bag and quickly left the office. She must find out more about the relationship between Swen and Jennie Kingsley and why these three obscure sites had been pinpointed on Swen's county map.

Today she still drove her trusty Land-cruiser. As she backed out into the street, she spotted Kingsley's foreman, Hal Barkley, entering the Lazy Z Tavern. This presented the perfect opportunity. Barkley was certain to know all about Swen's relationship with Kingsley's wife. If Barkley wasn't as loyal to the Kingsleys as everyone supposed, he might be willing to tell her all he knew.

The idea hadn't struck her until she had stepped into the bar: Barkley might actually be hired by Swen as an inside man, working for Swen instead of Kingsley. The thought caused her to draw to an uncertain halt.

Kate stepped further into the darkened interior, assailed by the smell of beer and greasy food. A crowd had gathered near a big-screen TV, loudly cheering a favourite team.

Kate, eyes adjusting to the light, looked around for Hal Barkley, but settled instead, on the familiar face of Jake Pierson. The museum curator, a half-finished hamburger before him, sat at a secluded booth some distance from the TV. Kate drew in her breath. Seated next to him was the man with the peroxide hair she had seen watching her at Pauley's Auction Barn.

Jake Pierson glanced up, an affable smile lighting his face. She watched as he lifted a plastic tray, scooped the remainder of his lunch into the waste bin, and strode toward her. Today the tied-back hair, the phony Western image, or maybe the company he kept, made him look at home in these dim, grungy surroundings.

'So what's a nice girl like you doing in this place full of ruffians?' he quipped.

'My job,' Kate replied. 'I'm looking for Hal Barkley.'

"Hal?' Pierson's alertly skimmed the room. 'I thought I saw him come in a while ago.'

As he spoke, Barkley appeared from the dark recesses of the bar with a mug of beer and slipped into the seat Pierson had just vacated.

'There he is,' Pierson said. 'He was lying in wait to steal my seat.' His voice lowered, although no one could have heard him anyway over the racket. 'Can't say I'm sorry. I ducked in to grab a bite to eat and catch the score when that character they call Slim sits down right next to me.' He gave a mock shudder. 'Like trying to eat with Billy the Kid. Enough to ruin my appetite.'

So now the surly cowboy had a name. Slim.

Barkley, leaning forward, said something to Slim that caused him to turn towards her. His long angular face — if possible — appeared even more cold and frightening than at their last meeting.

Kate, pretending not to notice, looked quickly back at Jake Pierson, who had by this time come back into focus as the kindly, educated man who had assisted her at the museum. 'Who is that man with Barkley?' she asked him. 'Does he work for the Rocking C?'

'Slim, that's all I know. In fact, from the sight of him, that's all I want to know.' Pierson's gaze, filled with concern, shifted back to her. 'He's sure giving you a murderous look. Do you think you should stay here?'

'I need to talk to Barkley.'

'I'll be glad to accompany you,' he offered gallantly. 'We can both go over there now if you like.'

'Thanks, but no need.'

As soon as the museum curator left, Kate headed to their table. Barkley, muscular arms propped on his elbows, seemed only half hearing what Slim was saying to him. A sharp frown cut between his brows. When he replied, it must have been not to Slim's

137

liking, for he was holding his ground in a mean, sullen way. His hair, pale in the dull light, looked purposefully bleached and hung in shaggy lengths across his denim jacket.

Kate, heart pounding, stopped at their table. Slim glared at her, the same way he had when he was spying on her at Pauley's Auction. More than ever, Kate was convinced that he was the one who had sabotaged her tyre, causing her to break down on that deserted road.

'You'd better not be following me,' he said in an undertone.

Barkley spoke harshly, 'She's here to see me.'

The blond man, a match for Barkley in combativeness, angrily grabbed his Stetson and left the bar.

'What do you want?'

Kate slipped into the seat Slim had vacated. Her voice rose, battling the shouting and the blare of the television as she said, 'We haven't really had a chance to talk. I need for you to answer a few questions.'

'Like what?'

'To begin with, how long have you worked for the Rocking C?'

'Two years, going on three. Long enough to hate those vipers at the Double S.'

'Where did you work before Mr Kingsley hired you?'

'I owned a little spread of my own between here and Laramie. Had to sell out.' He added, a bit resentfully, 'Too hard for the little guys to make a go of it in this economy.'

'How did you meet Charles Kingsley?'

'At a rodeo in Casper,' he replied. 'Slim, that guy I was talking to when you came in, rode the circuit then. Charles and I began making friendly bets on Slim's success. I usually won. Anyway, we got to be buddies, and Charles offered me a job. But what's that got to do with anything?'

'What can you tell me about your friend Slim?'

'I wouldn't exactly call him a friend. Slim's a fellow rancher. Runs the Bar 8 over near the Colorado border. I do a little business with him now and then, that's all.'

'What's his last name?'

'Barton.'

'What else can you tell me about him?'

'Slim worked for Charles once, but that was before I hired on. That's all I know about him.' He fell obstinately silent.

'I suppose you met Jennie Irwin in Casper, too.'

The mention of her name caused him to

brighten. 'I did. Little Jennie is a fan of anything Western. She loves horses.' He added proudly, 'Years back she was voted Casper's rodeo queen.' He paused, smiled, then added, 'Some little gal. I dated her myself a few times, but lost out the minute I introduced her to my boss.'

'What about Swen? Was he acquainted with her, too?'

'I hear he courted her once, or tried to. That fell by the way, lucky for her.'

'How long did they see each other?'

'However long it took her to find out how no-good he is. And not long after she met Charles. Jennie's friendly, but she doesn't play the field any. She's the faithful kind.'

So many possibilities existed, so many ways a clever person could take control of Kingsley's fortune.

'Charles did the right thing when he made me foreman,' he boasted. 'Jennie can depend on me.'

'You've been ranching most of your life, haven't you?' Kate asked. 'You must have had experience dealing with cattle rustling. Is there anything you can tell me about how a rustler works?'

Barkley frowned sharply as if she were accusing him, then he ran a work-hardened hand against his beard before he replied.

'Most of the scum I've run into are small-timers. They steal calves before they're branded. But what I'm up against here is a big-money man who's too slippery to take the fall himself. Swen had no earthly reason to be stealing from us, only vengeance. He'd go to any length to watch Kingsley sweat. He chuckled over being able to profit himself from Kingsley's loss.'

'But Swen claims to have missing cattle, too.'

'So he says. But he's the one who got caught red-handed. Charles found proof of his guilt and intended to go for his throat.'

'What reason do you have for thinking Swen's guilty?'

'Because I know,' Barkley replied, leaning across the table, 'just how they do it. They tear down their own fences, let their cattle run with ours. Then they load them up and take ours as well. Wouldn't be any trick to alter a brand from a Rocking C to a Double S. The last time I found a fence cut, that's when I went over there to have it out with them. Of course then I didn't know about the lawsuit Charles was filing.'

'What happened once you accused Swen?'

'He ordered me to get off his land and when I didn't, he turned that thug Garrison loose on me. I did a lot of defending myself.'

Kate still didn't know any more about who started the fight than she had before, although she had her suspicions. Barkley had trouble looking innocent, even now when he was making every effort to do so.

'What will happen to the lawsuit? Have you talked to Kingsley's lawyer?'

'The whole thing is dead in the water. Charles had just spoken to his attorney on the phone, but hadn't turned over the evidence. And none of us know exactly what proof he had.'

Barkley stared morosely down at the table, a frown cutting a deep line between his eyes. 'If you ask me,' he said bitterly, 'it's not over yet. Not even with Charles dead and buried. I think Ty Garrison has stopped following Swen's orders and has begun to work for himself.'

After Kate left the bar, she went directly out to Swen's ranch. An elderly housekeeper answered the door and left her standing on the porch for a long while before she returned. 'This way. Mr Swen is in his study.'

Kate's anxiety had grown during the long wait, but as she entered the house, she thought of the last time she'd been here, of Ty and of the warm comforting fire.

Swen was seated at a huge walnut desk before scatterings of ledgers and papers. The way he rose in such gentlemanly fashion caused Kate to picture him in an elegant suit rather than in dusty denims. She waited without speaking, expecting the same rudeness she had faced from the men at the bar.

Instead he asked quietly, 'How's Ben?'

'He's still in the hospital. The doctors keep running tests. So far they have come up with nothing. They're beginning to believe his problems must be stress related.'

'Or doughnut related.' Swen's smile made his lined face look less hard. 'What brings you here?'

'Unanswered questions,' Kate said. 'Do you mind helping me out?'

Swen sank back into the leather chair. 'Not in the least.'

'Who generally drives the truck that rammed into my squad car?'

'Mostly the help I hire for the house. The cook takes it to Rock Creek every Friday for supplies. Other than that, I guess Ty uses it the most.'

'And you?'

'Not often, but at times.'

'You told me that you always left the keys in it. That would make it accessible to, say, someone from the Kingsley's ranch.'

'Yes.'

'I'd like to know more about Kingsley's

foreman. Is there anything you can tell me.'

'Barkley ran a ranch west of Laramie, but drank and gambled and went belly up.' Swen added in the same even tone, 'Kingsley could never tell the sheep from the goats.'

'I've just come from talking to him. Of course, he thinks the thefts are coming from your ranch.'

'And I always believed the devilment sprang right from the Lazy C. Until recently, that is.'

'When I was here last, you were about to give me your opinion of what's been going on.' Kate waited, reading in his manner the fact that Swen no longer considered confiding in her. Jeff had ruined that.

'I've tried to work with the sheriff's department in the past,' he replied, 'with zero results.'

'But I'm the acting sheriff now. And I think we would both gain by joining forces.'

'Haven't you been in enough danger already? I don't want to involve you in any more.'

'You might be the one in danger, Mr Swen.'

'You don't have to warn me, Kate,' he replied, 'or protect me either. I always work solo and accept full responsibility for my decisions.'

Kate recalled what Barkley had said about the possibility of Ty's working for himself. Even though she didn't agree with him, she felt obligated to pose the question. 'What if this turns out to be an inside job?'

'Then I'll make adjustments. Recognizing the truth and facing it, that's what life's all about.' Swen's eyes held to hers, steady in his strong, weathered face. 'But don't worry. This isn't any double-cross by my own men. Kingsley didn't know the sheep from the goats, but I do.'

'I've noticed how closely you work with Ty Garrison. You've given him free rein. Do you. . . .'

'Ty's the best friend I've ever had,' he interrupted, 'so you can get off that track.'

Kate, reassured by his words that sounded so certain, settled back in her chair. 'Do you know a man named Slim Barton?'

'Yes. He worked for Kingsley several years ago. Another low life, always in and out of jail. A burned-out rodeo star who took to drinking. Alcohol and prison, that about sums him up.'

'Who does he work for now?'

'He runs a ranch of his own where he barely ekes out a living. He wouldn't have the brains or the initiative to pull off a large-scale scheme like this.'

'Could he be getting help, say, from Hal Barkley?'

'Barkley wouldn't go up against Kingsley. If the trouble is coming from the Lazy C, Kingsley instigated it. And we can't rule that out.' Swen was silent for a while, then added, 'Kingsley did everyone wrong, especially that little niece of his. By rights he should have secured the ranch for her, but I hear she's making plans to leave.'

'And that means Jennie Kingsley will be in full charge.' Kate had succeeded in bringing the subject around to her without making it obvious. 'I suppose you were acquainted with her before their marriage?'

Kate waited expectantly for Swen to answer and was glad when he didn't lie.

'Yes.'

'What's your impression of her?' Kate pressed.

'Jennie's a right nice lady,' Swen said. 'Certainly not a troublemaker or a thief. In fact, I don't know how she ever got mixed up with him.'

Kate had got this far. She had to know more. 'Did you date her before she started seeing Mr Kingsley?'

'Whenever I went to Casper, I'd call her to have dinner with me. We're friends.

That's all.'

'Did you see her on Monday, the day Kingsley was shot?'

The lines around Swen's mouth and eyes tensed. At the same time he pushed back his chair as if in abrupt dismissal. 'No, I did not.'

Aware of a slight advantage, needing to push him further on the subject Kate, on impulse, took out the county map. She unfolded it and placed it in front of him on the desk. 'Are you the one who wrote down these phone numbers?'

'Where did you get this?'

'From the glove compartment of your black pickup.'

'I wrote down the first two,' he said, 'but not the last. Why do you ask?'

'Because I find it odd that Jennie's phone number would be jotted down on your map.'

Swen's gaze remained lowered. Light glowed across his grey hair, highlighting the silver curls around his temples.

'What are those?' He indicated the three x's spaced inches from one another.

'Were you the one who marked those spots?' Once more she felt led to believe his certain answer.

'No, I didn't.'

'Do they have any significance to you?'

Swen studied the map carefully as if trying to imprint in his mind each exact location. 'I have no idea what they mean,' he replied shortly.

A decided change had come over him. Swen slid the map across the desk towards her, saying, 'That's about all the questions I have time for today, Kate. I've got an appointment to keep.'

The leaden gold of approaching dusk hugged the horizon as Kate drove towards Kingsley's ranch. Her hands instinctively tightened on the wheel as she approached the intersection of the two blacktopped roads where Swen's truck had sped toward her with such deadly force.

Kate made a sharp right turn towards the Rocking C. Enough daylight existed to check out the only x marked on Kingsley's property, a seldom, if ever used section of range high in the rugged canyon area.

She passed Kingsley's towering home and headed north on a narrow road past high fences and sprawling bunkhouses. Several miles beyond she spotted through a shield of cottonwoods and pines the old wooden-frame house where Kingsley's foreman lived. She caught no sign of activity. Barkley was probably still in the Lazy Z drinking.

The road seemed to go on forever in a

series of gently winding s-curves. Kate could see the tips of purple-hazed mountains in the distance, but all around her was grazing land interspersed by large boulders and tall, grey bluffs, like the set from some Western movie.

She drove several more miles until she hit gravel that soon gave way to a deeply rutted dirt trail. She could see no sign of civilization except for the barbed-wire fence that marked the dividing line between the adjoining ranches. Kate continued, aware she had entered the most isolated spot of the Kingsley spread. With an area covering over a hundred square miles, it was likely Hal Barkley seldom even got around to checking this part of the ranch.

The trail grew steep and treacherous. The Landcruiser jolted upward to a very lofty elevation. The flat terrain changed into granite ridges and forests dotted with aspen, their leaves glowing gold in the waning light.

Kate stopped at the top of the cliff. The road continued, a deeply eroded path dropping almost straight down. She pulled out the map to orientate herself, deciding she was still miles from the marked location. Because it would soon be dark, she would not attempt this precarious descent, nor would she set out walking.

Possibly another road existed, a more direct route to the edge of Kingsley's property. She would investigate that tomorrow. For now, she climbed from the car breathing deeply the pine-scented air. From her panoramic view she could see the sage-covered fields she had just crossed, spotted with yellow black-eyed susans and purple asters. Cutting through the cliffs to her left, Rock Creek wound snake-like across the flat range-land towards town. The water in places appeared motionless, deep and muddy.

When Kate turned to go back to her vehicle, she caught movement from the deep ravine below her. She shielded her eyes against the brilliant rays of dying sun and saw Swen. He walked with quick, sure stride, his hand loosely gripping a rifle.

Why was he on Charles Kingsley's property? She thought again of his abrupt dismissal. His 'appointment' must have had something to do with the x marked on the map. Swen had started out the moment she had left and taken a short cut to the site.

She had no choice but to find out what he was doing. Kate started down the steep bluff. By the time she reached the bottom of the slope, Swen had vanished into the thick trees.

Kate wandered cautiously through a deeply wooded area that continued to slant downwards. From the level ground below she caught the scent of cattle, mingled with the earthy smell of the creek. Kate didn't have to guess what was going on: this secluded spot was a hiding place where cattle were secreted onto waiting trucks. Probably Swen had come out here to warn his men that they had to act quickly for the sheriff would soon find their place of operation.

She halted behind a wall of pines and peered out into the clearing. A makeshift corral, fashioned from crudely chopped tree limbs, was crammed with cattle. Angled close to the gate set an ordinary-looking cattle truck, just like hundreds in the area. The back ramp was down ready to load, so she could not see the licence plate.

Had Jeff had been right, all along? Swen's being here on Kingsley's land made it seem certain that Swen, just as Kingsley had claimed, was the one stealing his cattle.

If so, Swen had come out here to meet with his crew. But where was he now, and where were the thieves who worked for him? Kate edged closer. As she did, someone inside the truck — someone who had spotted her — threw open the door. She caught a hasty glimpse of a rifle barrel. At the same time she heard a click as a bullet was being thrust into the firing chamber. Kate whirled around, plunging deep into the cover of trees. Even though she hadn't seen the gunman, the vision of Swen aiming a rifle at her increased her speed.

Feet scuffled and a slight curse sounded as the man broke though the trees behind her. Hoping to confuse him, she changed course, not once, but several times until she herself lost all sense of direction.

Still, he followed. Kate considered hiding, but knew he would only keep looking until he found her. Her only chance lay in flight.

Barely able to catch her breath, she tried to outdistance him. The swish of branches and the scattering of rocks warned her that he was in close pursuit. To make things worse, darkness, like an inky cloak, had begun to fall around her, obscuring both her vision and her judgment.

Gasping for air, with legs becoming too weak to hold her, she was forced to draw to a halting stop: the wrong thing to do. The moment she stopped moving, she had become a sure target.

A shot rang out. It struck the boulder beside her that rose, high and jagged, from a bed of rock. She jumped away from the path of the ricocheting bullet, then dived into a thicket of juniper, scampering on hands and knees until she was able to regain her footing.

What had possessed her to follow Swen when she wasn't even carrying a gun? How many men were out here? Chances are, they had her surrounded. Even if they didn't, they knew she would try to reach her vehicle and could easily track her down before she did.

Finally, too exhausted to keep up such a wild pace, she halted again. Another mistake! This time the bullet hit her. Wincing, grabbing her arm, Kate dived into the trees, falling flat on the ground into a sea of leaves. She dared not lift her head, dared not make a move. Running her off the road had been a warning. This time he meant to kill her!

The numbness in her upper arm quickly wore off, leaving a searing pain. She knew the bullet had just penetrated the surface of her skin: it was the gushing blood that worried her.

Kate waited, every sense alert. When she was sure he had passed by, she took a chance, sprang to her feet and ran. To her relief, she was very near the cliff, which rose, dark and looming, just above her. She had a chance to reach the top — to live! But her effort must be fast and sure for the absence of trees on the slope would leave her vulnerable.

Kate hesitated. She could do it. This thought, this rush of hope, increased her boldness, gave her new energy. She started off in a zigzagging course, not looking back, not considering the fact that she was now in plain sight. Miraculously she reached the crest of the hill. There she halted, afraid to take a step closer. The bonnet of her vehicle gaped open, cut wires and hoses hung loose from the motor.

Kate's heart sank. The rustlers had blocked her only means of escape. One of them had beaten her to her Landcruiser. No doubt they had taken her phone, too. But whether they had or not, she couldn't risk going any closer. Whoever had immobilized her vehicle, was certain to be lying in wait for her.

Her only concern of the moment was staying alive. She half ran, half slid back down to the canyon floor and began again her wild race to nowhere. She scrambled over sagebrush and thistle, hurrying to get out of range shot.

Kate, sick and disoriented, didn't know how long she fled through the underbrush, but slowly she became half-aware of the damp coldness, the sharp, pungent scent of sage.

It became increasingly harder for her to see, to keep her wobbly legs moving. As she started down a rough patch of rocks, her foot slipped, and she fell hard against earth and stones. This time she could not get up.

After a while with some trouble she lifted her left arm. Blood seeped through her pullover, lots of it, streaming down her arm, through her fingers. She was losing too much blood. Still, she could not afford to stop and bind up the wound. That might cost her life.

Using all the strength she had left, she struggled to her feet and stumbled on again. Dusk had given way to darkness, and only the light of the moon illuminated her way. Kate was hopelessly lost, but at least she could no longer hear the sound of footsteps behind or the snap of branches.

Again she had to stop, if only for a moment. She took refuge behind a clump of trees and rested. A rabbit darted into the sagebrush making her start, then total silence. After what seemed an eternity, she ventured a look around, seeing no one, hearing no sound but the gurgling of the nearby creek. Kate's entire body sagged with relief.

She had lost her pursuer.

Before she could rise again, she heard the rattling sound of a large, heavy truck. The rustlers could not afford to be caught out here with the stolen cattle, so at least some of them must have given up chasing her. But now she was faced with another problem. The thieves were gone, but she was out here all alone and fast losing blood.

A biting wind blew, causing a chill to settle over her. Kate shivered. She didn't know how badly she was hurt: she'd never been shot before.

Why did she always have to act on impulse? She had been wrong following Swen into the canyon, dead wrong, trying to work this case alone. She had been so self-assured. But no amount of police schooling had prepared her for her first real-life encounter.

Kate should have told Jeff where she was going. She thought of Ben, who had put such faith in her. Ben would be angry that she had fallen into this trap when she had promised him she wouldn't work again without backup. Kate gritted her teeth against the pain. If she lived through this, she'd apologize.

With the help of a tree trunk, Kate rose unsteadily to her feet. She felt light-headed, and knew she was dangerously close to losing consciousness. The water from Rock Creek rippling around boulders sounded loud. Just a few steps away, she told herself. She began to weave toward it: cold water splashed on her face might stop the increasing dizziness, might revive her, might make it possible for her to go on.

Kate could see the bank now, only yards away. Her vision blurred and began to blacken. Halfway to the water's edge, overcome with faintness, she slumped to the ground.

Kate awoke to penetrating cold and a throbbing between her shoulder and elbow that shot off waves of pain. Managing to turn to her side, she forced open her eyes and through hazy vision made out a pair of cowboy boots. She lifted her gaze and saw Ty Garrison standing over her, a revolver clutched in his hand.

CHAPTER 8

Even the sky behind its imposing frame looked icy, too clear, too stark. Light from a brilliant half-moon lit Ty's features, blending into them the same harshness. For a moment Kate held her breath, fearing she had been wrong about him.

'Kate, what happened?'

'The rustlers . . . I followed them here. They shot at me. A bullet struck my arm.'

Ty reacted quickly. He removed his jacket, then his shirt. He ripped off the sleeve and used it as a tourniquet. Then he wrapped his jacket, still warm from his body, around her. He slipped back into the sleeveless shirt and lifted her.

'I can walk,' she said.

'This is fine,' he replied, no change in his breath from the exertion. 'For a girl with an appetite, you don't weigh anything.'

Surprisingly, Kate felt safe pressed against him. She was aware of the tightness of his arms, the sureness of his steps. He carried her effortlessly, not up the cliff but continuing along the level ground beside the creek.

'How did you find me?'

'I was out checking on our fenceline. I spotted your Landcruiser. When I drove up there, I saw the damage that had been done. That's when I set out looking for you. I didn't want to risk the drive down into the canyon at night, so I took this lower route.'

He continued on with a slow but steady pace. 'Who shot at you, Kate? Do you know?'

It sounded as if someone answered for her in some strange husky whisper. 'I'm not sure. I didn't see him.'

'What did you see, Kate?'

'A truck about to load cattle.'

'Can you identify the vehicle? Get a plate number or a partial one?'

'I wasn't able to.'

Ty, supporting her, let her stand while he opened the truck door. Then he lifted her inside. This pickup smelled of new leather, not like the old one that had battered her squad car. Ty quickly started the motor and turned on the heater.

First it blew out cold air, air that slowly became wonderfully warm. Kate rested her head against the back of her seat and closed her eyes. She felt drowsy, suspended in some state of pain and half-awareness.

She could hear Ty speaking from some world she didn't inhabit. 'Are you doing okay? You just hang in there. I'm taking you to the hospital.'

Kate awakened to the scent of flowers. For a moment she felt confused and thought she was still lying out on the cold hard ground. She opened her eyes slowly to the sterile white walls and ceiling of a hospital room.

'So you're finally awake,' a nurse called cheerily, 'your boyfriend just left. He's been here most of the night. Refused to budge until he knew you were going to be all right.'

She must mean Jeff. The sheriff's department, of course, would be the first to be notified.

'He stayed, but you slept. I kept telling him you were heavily sedated, but he was sure something was wrong.' She slanted Kate a jolly look. 'You're one lucky girl, I'd say. He's so handsome and loyal. Not to mention romantic. He came back a while ago with these.'

Many people called Jeff good looking, but few would call him romantic. Kate edged herself upward, glimpsing the bouquet of wildflowers behind her on the windowsill.

Jeff had not been the one keeping the long night vigil. The events of yesterday slowly replayed. Once more, she felt Ty's strong arms lifting her, Ty carrying her along the creek bank to his truck.

At least she could still smile. Wildflowers were the only kind of flowers she liked and Ty had remembered. Yellow goldenrods in the centre flowed above an abundance of purple asters and black-eyed Susans. How sweet of Ty to take the time to gather them and bring them to her.

An elderly doctor poked his head into the room, saw that she was awake and entered.

'So when can I get out of here?'

He grimaced. 'You're just as bad as your boss. That's how Ben greets me every single morning.' He checked the gauze dressing on her arm. 'You were very lucky. The bullet made a clean entrance and exit. No permanent damage. Shock and loss of blood caused you to lose consciousness. In fact, Garrison found you at exactly the right time.'

'So I can leave?'

He considered her question with a thoughtful frown. 'I'm not like these fresh out of med school doctors. I don't believe in taking chances. No, I want you to stay so I can keep an eye on you. If everything looks

161

well, I'll release you first thing in the morning.'

'Why can't I go now? I feel fine.'

The doctor remained adamant. 'I've got one obstinate patient with Ben, I don't need two. You're staying until tomorrow morning. Doctor's orders.'

Kate lay back restlessly against the pillows. The day spanned endlessly before her. What a waste of time when she needed to be conducting an investigation, to follow up on last night's leads. Poor Ben, he had already been here a week and probably had another to go while he underwent a battery of tests. By now, he was probably fit to be tied.

'I can't just stay in this room all day,' she complained to the nurse when she returned.

'There's a little lobby at the end of the hall,' she said brightly, 'you can watch the big TV.'

Kate glanced down at the skimpy hospital gown. 'Like this?'

'I'll bring you a robe and slippers,' she said.

'Thanks,' Kate said, cheering.

She dreaded seeing Ben, who without exception never swayed from strict office rules. Trudging toward his room in slippers sizes too large for her, she felt as she had years ago when her little sister had pointed a finger at her and yelled, 'Kate did it!'

Ben sat up in bed, idly clicking the TV remote from channel to channel. He switched it off as she entered.

'I've been running relays back and forth to your room, but you were always asleep,' he said.

'They must have given me something that really knocked me out. How are you feeling today?'

'Ready to go home. But Doc has a zillion more tests lined up for me. I think he sits up nights thumbing through books on little-known diseases.'

'Better than surgery,' Kate returned lightly. Concerned, she added, 'You know, when you get out of here, you're going to have to watch your diet.'

'That's too much to ask of me, Kate. I'll never be able to do it.'

'You have to, Ben. You have to follow the doctor's orders. Not everyone gets a second chance.'

Ben shifted his heavy weight and adjusted the pillow at his back. 'You didn't come here to discuss my health.'

'No, I came in here to apologize for not following orders. It won't happen again.'

'You're right, it won't. What the devil were

you doing out on Kingsley property alone?'

'I was just driving around. I spotted Swen down in the canyon area with a rifle. I had to act fast or I'd lose him.'

'Too fast to call home?' Home, to Ben was the Belle County sheriff's office. The sagging folds around his eyes tightened and narrowed as he added in the same gruff way, 'There's no place on my staff for a cowboy — or girl. That type brings danger to everyone. You came within an inch of getting yourself killed.'

Ben looked sober and stern. For a moment, he reminded her of her father, upset and worried when she had returned late from a high school dance. He added, 'I heard Ty Garrison brought you in last night. Why do you think Swen and Garrison were on Kingsley property?'

'They could have been out there for the same reason I was: to catch the rustlers.'

'That's one explanation. I'm thinking of another. I'm beginning to think that lawsuit Kingsley was putting together against Swen had real teeth in it.'

'If Ty were guilty, he wouldn't have brought me into the hospital,' Kate insisted.

Ben slanted her a skeptical glance. 'That all depends on how he feels about you. I suppose cattle thieves are human too, at times.' He continued to watch her closely. 'You've gone too far, Kate, got yourself too personally involved.'

Maybe he was right, she had begun to like Ty far too much to be objective.

'I wish I were free to do my own work,' Ben exploded with great frustration.

'I'm handling everything the best I can, Ben. And don't forget, we're hot on the trail of the rustlers now.'

'And when we find them, Kate, we'll find the killer.' His statement reminded her of Swen's.

Ben's words, spoken with such certainty, caused an image of the invitation to Tom Horn's hanging to flash before her and once more she thought they didn't know the whole story yet. 'Maybe,' Kate responded, 'but not necessarily.'

'There's always scum to run down; that's why we're in business. But I'm not willing to trade catching any one of them — or all of them for that matter — for your life.' Ben paused significantly, the same paternal manner lining his face soberly. 'Jeff told me all about your date with Ty Garrison.'

Anger rose in Kate. She took a deep breath before she replied. 'I just happened to run across Ty in the café. Jeff knows that. He's manipulating everything, as usual, because he wants to be the one in charge.'

'Don't be so hard on Jeff,' Ben replied. 'He may be thinking of your safety.'

'Jeff doesn't. . . .'

Ben lifted a hand to stop her words. 'I ordered you not to go off on your own without backup. You did and got yourself shot. Even if you caught the cattle rustlers single-handed, you could expect a reprimand from me. As much as I hate to do it, Kate, I'm removing you as acting sheriff and putting Jeff in your place.'

Ben's quiet announcement, tinged with undercurrents of disappointment, hurt worse than the bullet that had struck her arm. She straightened up, trying hard to hide her reaction.

'I wasn't on duty,' she said. 'Doesn't that make any difference? What I do on my own time. . . .'

'Is still my business,' he finished for her. 'You were working my case.' The toughness in his voice faded, replaced by kindliness. 'Kate, I have to do this for your own good. Why, you're just a kid fresh out of school. I never thought you didn't have lessons to learn.'

Even though she knew Ben was protecting her, she still rankled over the thought that Jeff had won. He now held her position, the one he wanted most, acting sheriff in charge of the biggest case that had ever confronted Belle County.

Kate's resentment of Jeff grew as the afternoon wore on. Even though she knew better in her heart, she kept telling herself that Jeff's tattling to the sheriff about her and Ty had tipped the scales and cost her the appointment. How could he have run to Ben, twisting what he knew was her chance meeting with Ty into some romantic rendez-vous?

'Hi, Prep.' Jeff, a big smile on his face, strolled from the hallway toward her bed, placing a vase of pink roses on the stand beside her. The expensive green vase bore a golden tag reading, 'Betty's Floral.'

'So like you,' she said cuttingly, 'bringing flowers to someone you've just stabbed in the back.'

'You gave us all quite a scare,' he commented, ignoring her sarcasm. His worry, if that wasn't just some act, quickly dissipated into criticism. 'You know you shouldn't have been out there in the first place.'

'I don't need your lectures,' Kate returned coldly. 'What about my vehicle?'

'Someone, your boyfriend probably, cut it all up, mutilated the wires and hoses, but it's all taken care of now. Don't worry your pretty little curls about a thing.'

That infuriating lop-sided grin appeared again.

'That's the second vehicle you've ruined,' Jeff teased. 'I'm beginning to think you're working for Barney's Repair Shop instead of for us.'

As Kate smouldered, Jeff stepped to the windowsill, lifted the vase of wild flowers, and set it down again. 'Someone must be saving money,' he said. 'I should have thought of that myself. Plenty of them out in my cow pasture.'

He had the nerve, putting down Ty Garrison. Ty understood her in a way no one else did; he had brought her a gift she appreciated, one that spoke to her heart.

Jeff, despite her lack of pleasant responses, remained a long time making cheerful small talk. 'Better get back to work,' he said at last. He stopped at the door for one more smile, his close-cropped hair and skin looking dark against the surrounding white. 'Hurry and get out of here, Kate. We all miss you at the office.'

Kate had thought she wanted to be alone, but after Jeff left, her misery only increased: Ben and Jeff were right; she was wrong. She had failed them and deserved exactly what she got.

To add to her gloom, unanswered questions kept swirling around her, questions like why Ty and Swen were trespassing on Kingsley land, both fully armed. If Swen had been the one who had shot her, then Ty had taken a big chance going against his boss and bringing her to the hospital. Ty Garrison was either a hero working to help clear his employer's name, or a rustler who had risked his own cover in order to save her life.

When Kate entered the sheriff's office, Lem looked up from his desk. Because he usually failed to acknowledge Kate's entrance into the office, the grin that lit up his thin, lined face surprised her.

'I heard all about how you chased after those rustlers,' he said in an admiring way, 'how you took a bullet. You're all right, though, aren't you Kate?'

For the first time she seemed to merit the older deputy's approval. She returned his smile. 'I'm fine.' Her hand went automatically to the long sleeve that hid the bulky bandage. 'Arm's a little sore, that's all.'

'I think you're one gutsy gal, that's what I think!'

Kate basked for a moment in the praise which, coming from Lem, was comparable to being pinned with a medal, then she

169

asked, 'What's going on with the case?'

'We picked up Ty Garrison for questioning, but there's not enough evidence to hold either Swen or him. He made up a story about trying to hunt down the rustlers, said that's what they were doing that night. He told some wild tale about seeing a yellow-haired man in the canyon area.'

Slim Barton leapt to mind, the man Kate suspected of sabotaging the wheel of her car at Pauley's Auction. 'Could Ty make a positive identification?'

'No,' Lem said, 'he just got a glimpse of light hair.'

Lem rose, ambled over to the coffee maker, and filled a paper cup. 'Another curious thing, Jeff ran across that same man on the road the night you were shot. He stopped him near the canyon. He confiscated the .22 Winchester rifle Barton kept on a rack behind the seat of his truck.'

Lem went on with his accustomed slowness, 'We now have Barton's Winchester as well as Swen's old clip-style Marlin, and the pistol Garrison was carrying. If we could find a bullet or a shell casing to run through ballistics, we'd know which man shot at you.'

Finding such small objects in that vast, heavily wooded terrain sounded impossible, still, Kate decided that the first chance she got, she would hunt for evidence herself. After all, she would have the best chance of locating the places where the shots had been fired. Noticing that Lem was waiting for some response from her, she said, 'But so far we have nothing?'

'Nothing of importance.'

'Jeff and I went back out to the canyon this morning. All we could tell is that it looks as if they had taken that cattle pen down a time or two, as if they were in the habit of changing locations.'

'What about tyre tracks?'

'They must have done a speedy cover-up. The dirt around the corral had been swept clean. I think the shooter made it a point to retrieve the bullets and cartridge cases. He certainly wouldn't want to run the risk of leaving something behind that would point right to him.'

'So,' Kate began, 'the evidence is. . . .'

'Non-existent,' Jeff finished her sentence. He paused significantly, somewhat arrogantly, before he strode into the room.

'Or not found by us yet.'

Kate hadn't intended her statement to irritate him, but he gave a snappish reply. 'You're not the only competent one here. There's absolutely nothing out there. Regardless, it's no secret who shot you. Either Sam Swen, himself, or his accomplice, Garrison.'

'I'd like to take a look for myself.'

'We've had enough of your one-man,' he stopped, backtracked, and started again in the same surly way, 'we've had enough of your one-woman show. From now on, I handle things.'

Lem's slow drawl did nothing to soothe the mounting tension. 'You could just hear her out, Jeff. She's done a heap of a lot of work on this case.'

'Let's see, just what has she done?' Jeff ticked Kate's mistakes off on his fingers, 'Wrecked the squad car, dated the prime suspect, got herself shot. . . .'

Lem spoke up in her behalf again. 'Let's be fair, Jeff.'

'No, let's be truthful. We almost lost Kate because she can't follow simple orders. And because she can't, Ben handed her job over to me.'

How would she ever be able to put up with his insufferable attitude? 'Ben may have put you in charge, but he didn't take me off the case.'

Almost no one ever opposed Jeff, but now she had added her challenge to Lem's and that, she realized, had been a big mistake.

Jeff spoke acidly, 'Ben didn't take you off the case, but I am.' He turned his back on her and headed to his desk.

Lem set down his coffee cup, spilling liquid as he did. 'Stop it, Jeff, we've got enough trouble. We don't need you two bickering.'

Jeff addressed Lem as if Kate had left the room. 'She needs to learn to be a team player, or she's no good to us,' he said with great bitterness. 'Besides, what's she thinking, trying to go back to work already?' He directed his next words to her. 'Just go home.'

No reply she made would change his mind. Kate swung away from them and headed to the door. Jeff's words thundered after her.

'I'm putting you on leave for the next three days. And if I find you meddling in any way, you'll answer to me.'

Kate firmly closed the door between them, but that did not block out his words.

'You're off this case, and that's final. Consider yourself warned.'

Smouldering with resentment, Kate left the building and almost collided with Sam Swen.

'Whoa.' He drew to a quick stop, touching the brim of his hat, greeting her in an appealing, old-fashioned way. 'You must be hot on another lead.'

'I'm not, but are you?'

The two regarded each other, Kate picturing how he had looked that evening in the canyon, rifle in hand. She felt afraid of him, just as anyone who was foolish enough to get in his way.

'I'm just reporting into the sheriff's office like I was told to do. Jeff just won't give up, even though I've already told him everything I know.'

'You must have left your ranch Sunday evening the same time I did.'

'Yes. I went directly out to that spot on Kingsley's land marked with an x, the one you showed me. By the way, thanks for sharing that information. I'm sure no one expected me ever to lay eyes on that map.'

Another mistake of hers Jeff could add to his tally, Kate thought, but made no comment.

Swen went on, 'I kept asking myself: why would anyone mark my map and leave it in my truck? There seems to be only one answer.' His grey eyes narrowed. 'You may have been right when you suggested one of my own men might be involved. I may have hired a hand that works for Kingsley, albeit not a very clever one.'

Swen straightened his shoulders in a way that caused her to picture him aiming a rifle and pulling the trigger. 'He'll need heaven's help if I ever find him.'

'You can't. . . .'

'Can't what? Retaliate? Your question reminds me of a line from Macbeth, "Let us be beaten if we cannot fight".'

'Look what happened to Macbeth.'

'That was because of his wife,' Swen said, lightening a little, 'and I'm lucky enough not to have one.'

'You must have thought you would encounter someone on Kingsley's property that night. Which explains why you took a gun with you.'

'A man who goes to war takes a weapon.'

'It's not up to you to do battle. That's our job.'

'There's many ways to fight,' he replied. 'I'm working on something now that will work . . . eventually.'

'What?'

'You'll be the first to know . . . when it happens. In the meantime, I'd suggest you do some checking on Slim Barton, who is probably working with Kingsley's foreman. Barton's been buying up land along the Colorado border.'

Kate waited for him to go on.

'Lots of it,' Swen said, then added adamantly, 'You tell me, how a two-bit operator like Slim Barton, fresh out of the state prison without a penny is able to pay cash in hand for vast stretches of good pasture.' Swen paused, then added, 'I'd better go on in. You're not working yet, I suppose.'

'No.'

Swen started toward the building.

'Swen, you can't take the law into your own hands.'

'I won't need to,' Swen replied. 'Like Tom Horn, these rustlers will soon be weaving a rope for their own hanging.'

Feeling upset over the implications of Swen's conversation and over Jeff's decision to remove her from the case, Kate crossed the street to Tumbleweed Café and ordered a cup of coffee. She clamped her ice-cold hands around the warm mug and wondered what on earth she was going to do now.

How could she just give up this case, *her* case?

She had been thrilled when Ben had singled her out for leadership, as fit to be his replacement. That moment of success had crumbled around her and left her helpless to pick up the pieces. She couldn't appeal to Ben for he would only agree with Jeff. If she didn't comply with Jeff's instructions, it would mean she would be dismissed as a deputy in the Belle County sheriff's department.

Kate stared morosely from the window-watching, yet removed from the quiet early-morning lull. A woman hurried past the restaurant. Jennie Kingsley, Kate thought, noting the stylish Western hat, the short denim skirt and embroidered blouse and vest. No, this lady was too tall, too thin, and too young to be Kingsley's new bride.

The woman turned her head slightly, and with a jolt Kate recognized Mary Ellen. She must be taking fashion lessons from her new aunt. She had tinted her hair, for the light strands that escaped from her hat brim waved Jennie-style around her face. Hooped earrings, inlaid with turquoise, bobbed with every step. Kate stared at her, amazed. What a change from the shy, frightened person she had questioned at the ranch. Only the high-heeled boots, which made her gait colt-ishly awkward, were reminiscent of the old Mary Ellen Kingsley.

Where could she be going dressed up to the nines, as if for some important date? Curious, Kate paid for her coffee and left the café. She reached the street just in time to see Mary Ellen entering the Belle County museum.

Mary Ellen and Jake Pierson stood in the dim recesses near the displays talking in hushed voices. Kate caught Mary Ellen's words as she entered. 'I just don't like what's happening. I think I should have left right away.'

The curator reached out for her hand and squeezed it tightly. At that moment Mary Ellen looked toward Kate, her eyes, void today of glasses, becoming wide and startled.

'Hi, Mary Ellen, Mr Pierson.'

The curator dropped his hand quickly to his side. Mary Ellen forced a smile. Of course she had heard about what had happened to Kate, but she didn't mention it.

Today, plain Mary Ellen gave the illusion of beauty. At any rate, she had managed to elicit the special attention of the attractive curator, Jake Pierson. Kate looked from one to the other, realization sinking in. The clothing and new hairdo were obviously for his benefit. She had assumed Mary Ellen and her boss were just good friends, but the special smile she had seen pass between them made her see for the first time evidence of budding romance.

'What are you doing here?' Mary Ellen asked, seeming embarrassed.

Kate looked from one to the other. 'I just

saw you walking by the café, Mary Ellen, and thought it would save me a trip. I wanted to ask you about Sunday, the night I was shot.'

'Ask me?' Mary Ellen glanced fearfully toward Pierson, as if incapable of responding on her own.

'She wouldn't know anything about the whereabouts of anyone,' he answered protectively. 'Mary Ellen attended the annual banquet for the Historical Society that night, which didn't break up until around eleven o'clock.'

'I guess that's all I needed to know then. Unless you happened to have run into Hal Barkley or anyone who works for Kingsley's that night and can give them an alibi as well.'

Mary Ellen glanced at Jake Pierson again, as if for courage, before she answered, 'No, I didn't see any of them. Jake, I had better be going now. I only stopped by for a minute. I have to get back to the ranch.'

'Don't want to leave Jennie alone, do you?' the curator remarked.

'I've been making plans to move out,' Mary Ellen explained to Kate. 'Get a place of my own. But I just can't bring myself to do it right now.' Mary Ellen spoke sadly, as if she were making some huge sacrifice.

'When I told Jennie of my plans she got so upset. She begged me not to go. She said she just couldn't bear being alone right now.'

'How long do you intend to stay at the ranch?' Kate asked.

'Until Jennie feels comfortable about my leaving.'

Although Mary Ellen didn't glance toward Jake Pierson, she nevertheless addressed him as she walked to the door. 'Don't forget, Jennie told Hal she's changed her mind about selling off some of Uncle Charles' Western collection. I made a special trip in today so you would know. You should get your bid in first.'

Mary Ellen's words surprised Kate. Jennie, from what she knew about her, would never consider parting with a single item of the Kingsley collection.

'Quite a girl, that Mary Ellen,' Jake Pierson said, still gazing toward the door she had just closed. 'Here she is, willing to help Jennie when she wants so badly to get away from there.'

To Kate, Pierson's words had a ring of falseness. Selflessness and Mary Ellen didn't seem to pair off. In fact, Kate's first impression of Kingsley's niece was that she seemed far too self-centered to notice much that didn't directly concern her. Probably, her delay had more to do with some plan of her own that had temporarily gone awry.

'It sure was good of Mary Ellen to drop by today,' the curator said excitedly. 'She's always thinking of other people. She knows just how much I want that collection for our museum.'

Kate's gaze moved automatically to the portrait of Tom Horn. In the stillness his painted eyes seemed to be trying to communicate some unspoken message.

CHAPTER 9

Kate was doing the same thing again — going off on her own, disobeying direct orders. When Jeff got wind of it, disaster was bound to follow. Even knowing this, unable to stop herself she continued driving towards Kingsley's ranch.

According to Swen, Slim Barton was buying up land; according to Ty, a yellow-haired man had been working with the cattle thieves. If Swen and Ty weren't guilty, if what they claimed was true, then Slim Barton had been the man who had shot her. But from what Kate knew about Barton, he lacked the brains and initiative to mastermind such a large-scale operation. He had to be working with someone else, someone who knew the ins and outs of both ranches. Kate's thoughts turned to Kingsley's foreman, Hal Barkley.

Luck smiled on her. Near the barn sat a pickup truck with open bonnet. As she approached, Kate stopped to admire it: egg-shell blue with a tasteful silver Rocking C emblazoned on the side.

As she came around to the front, she saw first a jean-clad figure and a shock of blond hair. Because she had been thinking of Slim Barton, she drew in her breath sharply. But it wasn't Slim who appeared all happy and smiling from under the bonnet.

'Didn't expect to see me working as a mechanic, did you?' Jennie said, laughing. She laid aside a wrench and wiped greasy fingers on her jacket.

The sharp fresh air, the love of her work, added roses to her pale skin and a sparkle to her eyes. 'There's nothing this old gal can't do. I was born roping and riding and. . . .' she glanced down dubiously at the motor, 'repairing trucks. Charles called this one mine. Said the colour was much too sissified for him.'

'I'm looking for Hal Barkley. Do you know where I can find him?'

'He headed home. Said he'd be tied up there this morning. Say, I'm about to stop for a coffee break, won't you join me?'

'Coffee sounds good.'

Jennie slanted a concerned glance toward Kate. 'I heard about what happened to you. I'm sorry. I can't believe there's people like that in this world. But Hal told me he was up against a mean bunch.'

Sunlight flashed across Jennie's earrings, tiny golden horseshoes dotted with diamonds.

'I like your earrings,' Kate said.

Jennie smiled. 'Charles bought me these. I love earrings, but I've never had the guts to get my ears pierced, so they're the clip-on kind. I'm always afraid of losing them.'

Anyone who would wear those, Kate thought, would be sure to like the earring with the Indian design found in Swen's truck. 'I see you have a necklace to match.'

As Jennie proudly showed off the large silver horseshoe that hung from her neck, Kate knew she had been right in not mentioning the lost earring. A great possibility existed that the owner would not know where she had lost it and would someday, if it belonged to a set, wear the matching necklace.

Once inside, braced by strong hot coffee, Kate remarked, 'I ran across Mary Ellen in town today. She looked . . . different.'

'I saw her leaving. It's weird,' Jennie said. 'She says she's staying here for a while longer. But I don't know why. I actually think the girl hates me.'

'Hates you?' Kate echoed. 'Probably she's

just jealous. No doubt she wants to be popular the way you've always been.'

'She could be if she'd get rid of that scowl. She needs to get out, mix with people.'

Kate thought of the museum curator. 'I think she's dating someone now.'

'No, I doubt it. Charles used to say she'd dress up and stay away for long periods of time, just to make him worry about her. It's crazy the way she won't let go of the past. This animosity of hers has to do with Charles and springs from that drifter she loved so long ago and didn't get to marry.'

Jennie took a long drink and set the mug aside. 'Or maybe the answer is just plain weirdness. Do you know Mary Ellen was bent on breaking up every woman Charles even considered marrying? Why, you should have heard the terrible lies she started about Anna Marks. Mary Ellen finally succeeded in breaking them up. That's why Charles never even told her about us.'

'I can't imagine why you would ask her to stay on here then.'

'Ask her? I just don't want to toss her out, that's all. With so much room and money, that would be so heartless. But all she does is sulk around and spy on me. I wish she would leave. The sooner the better.'

Kate thought of the meeting at the museum, of Mary Ellen's words so contradictory to what Jennie was telling her now. She wasn't sure which one of them to believe.

Kate finished her coffee. 'I heard Mary Ellen telling Jake Pierson at the museum that you're planning to sell some of your late husband's Western memorabilia.'

'She's mistaken, then,' Jennie said, lips tightening in exasperation. 'Every item in that collection means as much to me as it did to Charles. I intend to take it all with me to my grave.'

Her choice of words under the circumstance caused Kate to cringe a little.

Kate studied her. Either Mary Ellen or Jennie was lying, but which one? Kate reminded herself that Jennie, a woman of the world, might be accustomed to relying on her sweet face, her innocent blue eyes to profit by being convincing.

Kate asked at last, 'Are you keeping Hal Barkley on as foreman?'

'Of course. Why on earth wouldn't I? Hal's a dear, takes all the burden from my shoulders.'

'But you know all about the cattle rustling that's been going on. Don't you have any doubts about Barkley?'

'No, Hal was Charles' right-hand man. Charles thought the world of him and vice-versa. Charles always maintained that Swen was behind this, but I never believed that either. Might be some outfit from far off, just zeroing in on the two wealthiest ranches in the area.'

'What do you know about a rodeo rider named Slim Barton?'

'I remember him, from a long time ago. Slim won prize after prize, but that was back in my Rodeo Queen days. In fact, Charles hired him occasionally, when Slim fell on hard times. The rodeo life is a short-lived one. When Slim got washed up on the circuit, he started drinking, heard he even served some time in prison. But I think he's trying to go straight. Slim has his own ranch about fifty miles south of here, near Colorado.' Jennie stopped, breathless, 'Why are you asking about him?'

Kate's reply was lost to the opening of the front door. Jennie and she listened to the clank of high heels as they neared the kitchen.

Mary Ellen, looking chic and modern, poked her head into the room, beaming at Jennie. 'How do you like my new outfit?' She flashed Jennie a saccharine smile. 'Just like the ones you wear.' She stepped inside, giving a little whirl. 'Thanks to you, I'm learning how to dress.'

Jennie's lips parted in surprise.

'I'll get changed now,' Mary Ellen sing-songed in a voice as chic as her new clothing, 'so I can help with dinner.'

They listened to Mary Ellen's steps ascending the stairs to her room.

Jennie shook her head, the movement causing light to reflect against her blond curls. 'Help with dinner? That girl lazes around here most of the day expecting me to wait on her. To top it off, that's the first pleasant words she's spoken to me since I moved in.'

Jennie sank into a pensive silence before she continued. 'And that last remark about buying clothes like mine. She's made all those purchases just to get back at me, probably heard what I said about her the other day. I know what Charles meant now about how ugly and brooding that girl can be. Really, Kate, I can't wait to see the last of her.'

More puzzled than before, Kate left the Rocking C and turned down the road that would take her to Hal Barkley's home. Even though she knew she shouldn't risk confronting Barkley alone, she drove in an obsessed way, as if she were powerless to do otherwise.

Who to trust and who not to? If she

believed Swen, Barkley had a reputation for drinking and for double-dealing, which led her to Slim Barton, the shady character she had met in the tavern, who could well be working with Kingsley's foreman to rustle cattle.

Barkley's house bore a look of neglect, the peeled white paint, the crumbling steps and rotting boards on the porch.

Kate skimmed the yard, a jumble of old equipment and outbuildings. The area to the side of the barn looked like a graveyard for old vehicles. A battered cattle-truck, too small to be the one she had seen the night of the cattle rustling, was parked close to a sway-backed shed.

Kate cautiously approached the door, stillness answering her knock. She waited, an eerie sensation of being watched steeling over her. Kate pounded on the door again, certain that someone stood inside, silently waiting, refusing to answer. Kate stepped back, glancing up towards the dark, upstairs windows. All remained hushed and motionless.

Kate thought about pushing open the door, but she did not. As much as she wanted to, she couldn't risk entering Barkley's house without a search warrant. Kate paused uncertainly, then headed back to her car.

A low, ominous voice, one that seemed to come from nowhere, caused her to stop. 'What are you doing here?'

Kate whirled around to see Slim Barton emerging from behind an old brown Chevy. The small, wiry man moved quickly toward her, blond hair stringing raggedly around his thin face. He looked even more evil than he had in the dim light of the Lazy Z tavern.

Kate, with sinking heart aware of the isolation, stood her ground. 'I didn't expect to find you here,' she said evenly, as if trying to convince him or herself that she had nothing to fear.

Kate expected hostility, but Barton seemed to be making a grudging effort to be friendly. 'Me? I drove all the way out here to look at that old boat motor Hal has for sale.' He shrugged. 'Should've known it'd be a wasted trip. Hal ain't ever here.' His thin lips stretched, but fell short of a smile. 'Or if he is, he's not answering the door.'

'Do you know where he might be?'

Sullenness crept back into Slim's voice. 'How would I know? Do I look like his mother? He's probably down at the bar.'

Feeling uneasy even though no threat had been made, Kate lost no time getting into her Landcruiser and leaving Barkley's property. Slim Barton's cold eyes remained on her as if from behind the sights of a gun.

Intending to connect with the road that would lead her back past Swen's ranch, Kate turned north. She had just stopped at a crossroads when what she saw blotted out all thoughts of Slim Barton. She waited, clutching the wheel. Just ahead of her a pickup truck, eggshell blue, was passing under the Double S sign. She got a flash of blonde hair and caught a clear glimpse of the silver Rocking C marking on the side.

Why was Jennie Kingsley going to Swen's ranch? Answers swarmed around her. Swen and Jennie could have plotted this all along intending to end up with all of Charles Kingsley's estate.

Kate drove closer, pulling to a stop behind a shield of trees.

If Jennie and Swen married, Swen would be in control of not only the Double S, but also of his sworn enemy's ranch, the Rocking C. That would not only make him the richest rancher in Wyoming, but would also satisfy any desire the man might have had for vengeance.

But that wouldn't be the only possibility, Kate reminded herself. Jennie could be working on her own or working with Barkley or Slim. Her next step could be to marry Swen, who had dated her in the past and was probably already half-smitten with her. Maybe in the end she intended to kill Sam Swen too, and own the whole valley herself.

Kate peered through the branches at the old colonial-style mansion so much like Kingsley's. Swen himself, silver-haired broad shouldered, answered the door. Jennie, in a happy familiar way slipped past him into the house.

A calculating gold-digger, is that what she was? Had she married Charles Kingsley for his money, then shot him in cold blood? Swen might need more protection from Jennie than from the cattle rustlers, who could also be working for her. Kate thought of Charles Kingsley, lying dead in his study and of the vast fortune that had overnight become Jennie's. She thought of the stone that had been placed purposefully under Kingsley's head as if its very presence served some mocking, sinister purpose.

Whether Jennie was working alone or with someone else, it was beginning to look as if Kate had been on the wrong track today. Instead of checking out Hal Barkley, she should have been focusing instead on Kingsley's new widow.

Forgetting her injury, Kate rolled over on

her side to answer the phone. 'Kate Jepp.'

'Good Morning, Kate.'

She immediately recognized Ty's voice. More aware now of the catch in her breath rather than of the pain in her arm, she replied hesitantly. 'Ty, I've been meaning to call you. To thank you for . . . for everything. I loved the flowers.'

'I knew you would. How are you feeling?'

Again she paused, then said not too truthfully, 'Back to normal.'

'Good.' Ty's tone seemed to change midword, to become very serious. 'I must see you today, Kate. It's extremely important. Could you drive out to Swen's stables? You know where they are, don't you? At the very end of the Double S land.'

Doubts assailed her, but before she could reply, Ty said, 'I'll expect you there by tenthirty.'

Ty had hung up much too abruptly. Something must be wrong or else he had new information he intended to share with her. Kate hurriedly showered then rummaged through her clothes for a warm sweater and ran a brush through her tousled, dark hair. Kate knew she should not meet with Ty since Jeff had taken her off the case. She put aside her qualms. This meeting might turn out to be very important.

Kate was pleased to find the air outside warm and mellow. The haze of Indian summer hovered across the pastures, inflamed the trees along the draws with the brilliant colours of glowing fire. She drove past Swen's ranch then on for mile after mile. His stables were part of a complex of steel buildings and sprawling bunkhouses, all enclosed by a white fence and a sign that read Double S.

Ty, inside a corral, was attempting to rein in a very ornery looking horse that resisted like some balky old mule. 'Over here,' he called.

The horse, like in truce, temporarily stopped his battle then began stamping as if he were not satisfied with her slow advance.

'Kate, this is Drifter.' The horse made a snorting noise and shook his head: a wild-looking creature, big-boned heavy and grey, definitely not the sleek white Arabian horse she had pictured for Ty.

Kate reached out to pat the animal's rough, unattractive head.

'Careful. He doesn't like anyone but me. And not even me most of the time.'

'Where did you find him? Not in Arabia, I'm sure.'

Ty laughed. 'Actually I adopted him from the BLM wild horse program. We're just alike, us two. Most of the time he runs free, but once in a while we hang out together.'

'What did you want to talk to me about?'

Ty did not answer at once, almost as if he had some particular reason to delay. 'I thought we'd go for a horseback ride first. Would that be okay with you?'

Kate should say no; riding through the canyon with Ty was not part of her job description, but she brushed aside her doubts, smiled, and replied, 'I'm not riding Drifter.'

'I have the perfect one for you.' Ty dropped Drifter's reins and sorted out a gentle little mare. 'Her name's Chestnut. She'll love you.'

Kate watched as he saddled the horse he had chosen for her. An improvement over Drifter, with coat pretty and glistening.

'Need help?'

'No.' Kate reached for the saddle-horn, placed a foot in the stirrup, and pulled herself up.

'A pro,' Ty said.

Chestnut moved from the corral without any prompting. Ty struggled getting Drifter through the gate, then he stopped to latch it behind him. He swung up on the saddle, Drifter reacting with an irritable dance step. 'Follow me,' he said. 'We'll head up that high slope and down to the creek.'

Kate liked trailing after him, liked to watch his straight form, his natural poise against the jostling upward steps.

'In May this hill is bright red with Indian Paint Brush,' he said over his shoulder.

The lull of the jogging saddle, the fresh air around her, made Kate momentarily forget the continual trouble that had plagued her. Something healing about the high desert, she thought and felt almost happy. 'Ty, look at that? Goldenrod everywhere.'

'My favourite.'

The tall, graceful stems made her think of the vase of flowers she had taken home from the hospital and placed beside her bed, flowers Ty had gathered, arranged and brought just for her.

The sun began to make itself felt as they started down the sharp descent into another wide valley, this one dotted with mottled grey rocks and sage.

'The sky is so blue here,' Kate said. Many artists must have tried to paint this landscape, to capture the exact hue of a Wyoming sky feathered with clouds. She imagined most of them had given up in frustration.

'Hard to believe it will soon be winter,' Ty said.

'I dread the snow.'

'Mustn't do that. Winter's beautiful, too. The sun shining across white fields somehow lifts the spirits, gives you the heart to brave the cold.'

She could grow very fond of Wyoming, even think about making it her permanent home. Yet if she lost her job — because of actions like this one — her family would pressure her to return to Michigan.

'There it is, Rock Creek. Here's where we stop.'

Ty dismounted near the tall pines in the draw, came back to her and lifted her down. Once her feet were on solid ground, she thought again of the reason she was out here. 'Is this where we talk?'

'Yes it is.'

'What did you find out? What do you want to tell me?'

Ty did not let go of her, but drew her close. She could feel his muscular body pressed against hers, his strong arms holding her tightly. 'What I have to tell you is very important, Kate,' he said against her hair. 'The most important thing that I've ever said. I can't stop thinking about you.' He held her away from him for a moment, smiling into her eyes, sunshine falling across his handsome, rugged face. 'This is a very serious sign. I don't know, but I think it might be the first symptom of falling in love.'

Kate was too surprised to answer, but she didn't have to. Ty's arms encircled her again and this time he kissed her. His lips, gentle yet exciting, caused in her an unexpected response. She felt giddy, exuberant, like some teenager experiencing first love.

'We're not far from where we were Sunday night,' Ty told her. 'If you want me to, I'll show you the place where the rustlers cut our fence.' Ty glanced back at the horses contentedly grazing in the shade of a huge cottonwood. 'I think it would be easier to just walk from here.'

Ty caught her hand as they set off following the creek, which did not absorb the sunlight, but looked still and murky. They became surrounded by tangles of thick underbrush and twisted branches that rose from out of the muddy, shallow water. Although they were only a few miles from Swen's stables, Kate felt as if she had entered some alien land.

'How long have you known Hal Barkley?' Kate asked him.

'He has worked for Kingsley for some time, on and off. About two years ago Kingsley made him foreman.'

'And you've fought . . . often?'

'He hates Swen with a passion. Sometimes I have to step in and shut him up.'

That accounted for their fight; Barkley had come to Swen's, cursing, belligerent, probably even drunk. Of course Ty had intervened. Neither he nor Swen would be ones to call the sheriff's office instead of handling the situation themselves.

'I suppose Swen told you about the map I showed him,' Kate remarked.

Ty released her hand so quickly she felt as if she had said something wrong. 'Yes, and he's beginning to think one of rustlers might be working for him.'

'You have no idea who made the x's or why Jennie Kingsley's phone number was jotted in the margin?'

'No. Unless it was done by your attacker the night he stole our truck.'

'But why would he want to do that?'

'To make Swen look like the cattle rustler. To make it look as if he has direct ties to Jennie Kingsley.'

'I heard they did date before her marriage.'

'You're on the wrong track,' Ty insisted. 'Swen doesn't double-deal.'

Kate hoped he was right, but her doubts seemed to float in the air, as strong as the noises of the creek.

Ty stopped where a little waterfall trickled over rocks. The rushing of the stream told her this must be near the place she had fallen the night she had been shot. The gurgling noise, the same sound she had heard that night, brought a chill to her.

'Swen told me he was working on a plan that may trap the rustlers,' Kate said.

Ty hesitated. 'That's what I wanted to talk to you about. I trust you, Kate. I believe Swen is wrong about not bringing you in on this.'

Ty seemed on the verge of confiding something to her. Kate waited, reluctant to say anything that might cause him to change his mind.

'The thieves have been changing our brand, and they've been getting away with it. About a month ago, when we first suspected rustling, we started embedding microchips into the hides of some of our cattle.'

'Good thinking,' Kate replied. 'Since you've always used branding, the thief will not suspect you've started using another identification method.'

'Swen and I have been watching the cattle

200

auctions. So far, none of the microchips have turned up, but I think it's just a matter of time.'

'If any of your cattle do show up, once the State Brand Inspector reads the chip, the consigner, the thief, can be identified.'

They walked on.

'Where did you see the blond man who was out here?' Kate asked.

'I caught a glimpse of him here before he slipped into the cover of those trees. I tried to follow him, but soon lost his trail.'

Ty pointed out to her where the barbed wire had been slashed and pulled away. He crossed the fence line, saying, 'We're on Kingsley land now.'

The terrain began to look familiar. Kate could look straight up and see the cliff where she had parked the Landcruiser. Ahead of them sage and grass-filled pasture land was flanked by grey bluffs.

The steep ravine that held the secluded corral wasn't far away. Ty had not told her he intended to bring her here. Ty and Swen were the only people who had been proven to be out here the night she was shot. Filled with misgivings, she dropped further behind him.

'Not far now,' Ty said, the sound of his voice making her doubts vanish. 'The going's a little rough so watch your step.' Stones crumbled beneath their feet as they made a sudden descent onto the isolated valley floor.

With a shudder, Kate's gaze settled on the makeshift corral. As she wandered closer, the scent of cattle wafted up from the dry earth.

'I knew you were going to make a trip out here on your own,' Ty said. 'Thought we might as well join forces. Let's go over the area together, see what we can find. The rustlers must have left some clue behind.'

Kate knew she should doubt him, but strangely she felt safe. And being here would give her a chance to look for a bullet or shell casing. The location where the gunman had shot her, because it was set in a spot easy to find just below where her Landcruiser had been parked, would be the place to start. 'I'm going to head towards the cliff,' she told Ty.

'I'll be along shortly,' he answered. Ty had dropped back, kneeling, examining the ground as if he had found something that interested him, possibly tyre tracks. 'Don't stray too far.'

The air cooled as she passed into the shelter of the trees. A shiver ran through her as she thought of the cattle rustlers, of one in particular, the nameless man who had stalked her with a rifle.

Her task appeared hopeless. Jeff and the sheriff's crew had already scanned the canyon and had failed. Anyone would, in an attempt to uncover small objects in such a large wooded area where one clump of trees looked identical to another.

She followed as direct a course as she could, winding through endless mazes of pines and aspens. Apprehension grew the farther she got from Ty and the corral. She thought of turning back, but pressed on, determined to complete her search.

Prompted by her ever-increasing sense of uneasiness, Kate speeded her steps. As she did, a noise — like a footstep falling on dried leaves — crackled from behind her. She stopped, turned back, and listened. It must be Ty catching up with her. She waited, every sense alert, but time passed and he did not appear. No other sounds followed. Satisfied that what she had heard was just a deer or some small scampering animal, she headed on.

Kate recognized the area immediately, for she had fled from her place of hiding into a small clearing. Either the strain of the horseback ride or the remembrance of that sudden zing from the flying bullet caused a sudden, throbbing pain to start in her arm.

Finding the exact spot where the bullet had hit her had been so easy that she knew the gunman had probably found it, too. She took her time, combing the ground around the junipers she had dived into. He had been close to her when he had fired the shot, probably within twenty feet. She paced back to where she thought he had been standing and examined that area, too. Nothing. Likely, he had been here before her and had already removed the evidence.

But would he be able to locate the scene of the first shot? She didn't think so. Trees and darkness would have prevented him from seeing what she had seen. The bullet had struck a jagged rock and its odd shape had stayed in her mind. With any luck she could locate the stone again, find the nick in it, and trace the course of the bullet.

Kate wandered around for a long time before she stopped with certainty. She recalled how she had headed uphill and seen this very boulder rising from a flat bed of rock. Kate started toward it, but stopped at the rustling of branches from the slope just below her. For a moment she envisioned a gunman halting, lifting his rifle.

'Ty?' she called, but no answer came. Once again she reminded herself that the hillside was alive with many forms of life.

Kate turned full attention back to her search. She inspected the rock and found, dead in the centre, a small chip. She recalled how she had jumped back out of the path of the ricocheting bullet. It had barely missed her. She had thought at the time that it had hit the tree trunk just to her left.

She moved over to it and was able to locate the tiny tell-tale mark where the bullet had struck. It had lost the force to penetrate the bark of the aspen and so must have dropped to the ground close by. On hands and knees she used her fingers to brush through the debris. After a long search, surprisingly, she found a small portion of badly damaged bullet.

Her heart pounded. On fired bullets and cartridge cases no two firearms — even those of the same make and model — produced the same unique marks. She had won, had been able to come up with almost certain proof, with the 'mechanical fingerprint' that would lead them to the shooter.

Eagerly Kate lifted it from its bed of leaves. But as she examined the small object she held, disappointment drove away her rush of joy. The bullet was so fragmented, she wondered if it would be of any use to them. It looked as if it wouldn't have sufficient rifling impressions to match with those contained in the gun's barrel.

But if the gunman hadn't found this bullet, chances are he hadn't found the cartridge case either. Stuffing her find into her jeans pocket, Kate stood up. She hurried to where she supposed he had been standing at the time the shot was fired, and began an avid search for the shell casing. Being larger, it was much easier to find than the bullet. Again Kate felt a sense of elation.

Strong evidence, if it happened to match Swen's rifle or the one belonging to Slim Barton or Ty. She slipped it into the pocket of her jeans just as Ty emerged from between thick trees.

Kate stared into his eyes, shadowed by the overhead branches. He might have been standing there for some time, watching her. She half expected him to demand that she turn over to him what she had found. Unable to meet his steady gaze any longer, afraid she had led him to the evidence he could not track down himself, she turned away.

'You've been searching for a long while. Did you find anything, Kate?'

She avoided his question by reforming his, 'Did you?'

'At first I thought I'd found something,' Ty said, looking disappointed. 'But it turned out to be only a chunk of wood. I've scoured the entire area. Apparently they left no clues behind.'

As much as she wanted to trust him, Kate could not risk telling him about the bullet and cartridge she had hidden in her pocket. Anxious now to return to Rock Creek, to start the ballistics check, she said, 'I'm ready to go back.'

'I know a shortcut,' Ty said, taking her arm and leading her in the direction of Swen's land where they had left their horses. As the way narrowed, she went first, ahead of him. He walked slowly, stopping here and there to look back the way they had come. His delaying seemed almost deliberate, or was it just her nerves?

Kate recalled the sound she had heard on the trail, like footsteps crunching down on dry underbrush. She wondered if Ty had heard, too. He might have sensed someone was following them.

When they reached the creek, he stopped walking, gripped her shoulders, and looked deeply into her eyes. 'These people we're dealing with might be very dangerous. Be careful, Kate.'

Did he know about the evidence she was

concealing from him? In the stillness she thought of Ty standing over her that night with a revolver in his hand. She slipped out of his grasp. Nothing, not even her own reactions, made sense to her anymore.

CHAPTER 10

On the drive back to town Kate's apprehension grew. Periodically she glanced into the rear-view mirror and surveyed the vast stretch of emptiness behind her. The sight, which should have been reassuring, only caused a replaying of Sam Swen's warning, 'Trouble is, you don't see people like that. But they see you.'

Even though Kate had driven this same remote road many times since Kingsley's murder, today it looked ominously deserted. She pressed harder on the accelerator. The grazing cattle, the trails that cut off from the blacktop and wound through tree-lined gulches, appeared to her in a sort of unreal blur of speed.

Soon she must face Jeff, but even that didn't dull her sense of urgency, her anxiousness to turn the evidence she had found over to him. She already knew he would be angry. Why wouldn't he? She had flagrantly disebeyed his direct orders, but she hoped Jeff would weigh that against the fact that she had succeeded. What she would hand over to him would surely supply the proof needed not only to identify the man who had shot at her, but also the cattle rustler and likely the same man who had killed Charles Kingsley.

Furthermore, she had kept her find a secret. She had acted professionally, hadn't taken into her confidence Ty, even though she was tempted to do so. Jeff would have to give her some credit for that. Still the knowledge that Kate had played the role of a good sheriff didn't keep her from wishing that Ty was here beside her. She slowed for a curve, and as the vehicle straightened again, her tense grip on the wheel relaxed a little.

Kate had driven several miles before she spotted a car that had run off the road. An old, faded brown Chevy set immobile, smashed against a tree. She could see even from this distance that the bonnet had crumpled from the great impact.

Kate's heart sank. She had joined the department because she loved the challenge of investigating, of bringing justice and order to a community, but she detested this part of her job. She approached the wreck with dread. The car, spotted with rust and corrosion, looked as if it belonged in some junkyard. It had been driven hard under bad conditions. Mud spattered across the back, across the licence plate. The driver though, must be a local, for travellers rarely — if ever — ventured from the main highway onto the criss-cross of rough country trails.

As she pulled to a stop, Kate glimpsed the driver slumped behind the wheel. A person in danger — even without badge, gun, or ability to call the station — Kate must act quickly in the victim's best interests. She leapt out.

She hoped he wasn't badly hurt. She could see no reason why he had run off the road, unless he was drunk or had suffered a heart attack. Either way, his plight took priority over her own mission, which just moments ago had loomed as all-important.

Kate hastened towards the window, which was rolled down on the driver's side. He must be a ranch hand, for he wore a battered bulky black jacket and a cowboy hat. Her words rang out hollowly as she called, 'Sir, are you all right?'

No movement. She stepped closer, reaching out to touch his shoulder. Just as she did, his head jerked up.

The features beneath the cowboy hat were

obscured by a dark ski mask. He stared at her, his eyes through the gaping holes, narrow, colourless slits. The grotesque combination of ski mask and cowboy hat caused her to recoil with a startled cry.

With a rapid movement he lifted a revolver from the seat beside him. The small gun looked lost in his large hand. Despite the clumsy glove, he handled it like an expert, training it on her in a steady, menacing way. Kate, horrified, stumbled backwards.

'Stop, right there.'

His low, raspy words had a muffled quality, as if he intended to avoid the possibility of Kate's recognizing his voice. That could only mean one thing: at some point during her investigation, they had met.

He aimed the gun at her heart.

Fear caused weakness to wash over her. She had been set up, waylaid. An absurd image sprang to mind of a gentleman bandit holding up a train. But there was nothing make-believe about this man or his intentions. Deadly serious, dangerous: Kate was facing the rustler who had shot her once, and who would not hesitate to shoot again.

She remained staring at him, too fearful to move, frozen in place.

He hunched low in the seat with those terrible narrowed eyes fastened on her. 'I'll take that bullet and shell casing.'

Kate had no choice: either hand them over or die. With trembling fingers, she reached into her pocket and reluctantly placed the evidence into his outstretched hand.

She couldn't see his face, yet she was aware that he was smiling, smiling like the victor in some game of wit. The gun, which had momentarily lowered, rose again. Kate drew in her breath. He had what he wanted, but he intended to kill her anyway.

An explosion cracked, resounding around her. A bullet zinged by her striking the left front tire of her Landcruiser. The sound of expelling air mingled with his short triumphant laugh.

The battered Chevy she had thought incapable of moving roared to life. Kate, sick and dizzy, watched the dirt toss out from the spinning wheels as it pulled back onto the road. With her vehicle out of commission, she had no way of following him. All she could do was watch him speed off in the direction of town.

She worked with great haste, gasping for breath as she changed the flat tyre. As she sped toward Rock Creek, she blotted out all thoughts of the clever ruse. She didn't remember the details of driving back to town, only of skidding to a stop in front of the sheriff's department. With still-thudding heart, she rushed inside.

Lem in a startled way listened as she poured out the whole story. 'He never left the car so I couldn't judge his height. He wore a bulky jacket and a ski mask. Even though he had gloves on, I could tell he had big, strong hands.'

'Can you identify the voice?'

Kate shook her head. 'Disguised. It had a toneless quality.'

'Could it have been a woman?'

All along Kate suspected that a woman had driven the truck that had wrecked her squad car, but the person who had waylaid her today was definitely a man. 'No, not possible.'

Lem lapsed into silence, one soon filled with disbelief. 'You mean you didn't even get suspicious when you saw the licence plate covered with mud?'

'I . . . I thought someone needed help. I didn't think. . . .'

'You sure didn't.' Lem reached for the phone and called for their patrol cars to be on the lookout for a fifteen to twenty-year-old brown Chevy covered with rust and mud. He gave directions where it was last seen and ended with a firm warning, 'The driver is armed and dangerous.' Lem replaced the receiver. 'The way you describe the car, it probably came from some junk-yard. Or else it had been left abandoned.'

'If it is legally registered,' Kate agreed, 'it won't be to the driver. I noticed a lot of old cars out at Hal Barkley's place.'

'We'll check, but the perpetrator has to be one of those three men whose guns we're holding.' For a long time Lem did not continue. 'With no ballistics test, we've got nothing. Only a choice between Slim Barton, on one hand and Swen with Garrison working for him, on the other.'

'All we really have,' Kate said, 'is this: whoever fired that shot knew that I'd be looking for the evidence that would incriminate him.'

'That makes sense. Because of the darkness and the chase, he couldn't locate the place where he had shot at you, but he figured you could . . . and would. That's why he decided to keep an eye on you.' Lem paused thoughtfully. 'Or else he intention-ally lured you to the site counting on the fact that you would lead him to the evidence.'

'What I can't understand,' Kate said, 'is how he got ahead of me and staged this ac-cident so quickly.'

'Garrison and Swen working as partners,'

Lem suggested. 'You say you and Garrison weren't together for a long period of time? He probably planned to leave you free to search so he could watch you. At some interval he called Swen on a cellphone, and Swen either went himself or sent one of his henchmen to set this trap for you.'

Kate sank into the chair opposite Lem's desk remembering, although she tried not to, the feel of Ty's arms around her, the look on his face when he thought she was seriously injured. She could no longer concentrate on Lem's monologue, that slow drawl of his that continued even without her participation. The train of his thought appeared to be summed up, though, in one statement that jolted her back to the present.

'You had the evidence, then you lost it!' Lem groaned. 'I can't believe this! You went out there all alone, after all your warnings not to!'

'Ty called me. Then the rest . . . just happened.'

Lem's narrow features changed: the lines in his lean face became grim and tight. 'You're in serious trouble, Kate. What you've done is put your job on the line. Ben is a stickler for rules, you know that. And Jeff, he's even worse. Neither of them will budge an inch.' Lem added sadly, 'We both know what's going to happen now. And it would have, even if you had succeeded in bringing in the evidence. What on earth possessed you to go out there?'

'I thought it was worth the risk.'

'I don't think you deserve what Jeff is going to hand out to you,' Lem said. He remained silent for a while, then as if struck by a plan, spoke slowly and carefully, 'Whatever evidence you found is lost, so what have we got to gain by telling them? Let's just keep this between you and me. I'll have the boys maintain a lookout for that car, and when it's found, I'll handle it.' He leaned across the desk and his voice became louder, more adamant, 'Jeff doesn't need to know anything about what you did today.'

'So Jeff doesn't need to know?' Jeff burst out. He stormed into the office just as he had during their last encounter, his face flushed and angry. Obviously he had heard the entire story before entering the room. He glared at Lem. 'I'm going to tell Ben your exact words. We'll see if he reacts to them the same way I do.'

'She's inexperienced,' Lem muttered, gazing down sheepishly at the desk. 'And, Jeff,' he added hopefully, 'she almost pulled it off. I don't see why we can't cut her a little slack.'

'You're not in charge Lem, I am. I thought I knew you better. Here you are, willing to lie to me!'

'He wasn't going to lie.'

'No he just wasn't going to tell me the truth!' Jeff swung toward Kate. 'He was going to remain silent. The same difference, isn't it?'

Kate rose from her chair. 'Jeff, I. . . .'

'No use going over it again. I heard everything. You were snooping around on Kingsley's property. Against my orders, you headed right out to the crime scene. To top it all off, you took a major suspect with you!' Jeff's words continued hostile, unwavering. 'It all comes down to this: you found crucial evidence and lost it. You bungled and now the proof we need so badly is in the criminal's hands, not ours!'

'That happens sometimes,' Lem interceded, trying to defend her.

His statement, however mild and weakly spoken, unleashed Jeff's full fury. 'I suppose it didn't matter to you at all that you were taken off the case.'

Jeff stepped closer to Kate, his big form appeared to her like some solid wall that would remain in place, blocking all options.

'Well, this time, Deputy Jepp, you've gone way too far. You've left me no other choice.' In a voice that would tolerate no argument, he said, 'As of right now, I'm putting you on suspension. Turn in your badge and gun.'

Later that afternoon Kate returned to the sheriff's department. Jeff, not speaking, gestured for her to follow him into Ben's office. He accepted her gun and badge. He wasn't angry, only weary and a little sad.

'I want you to know, Kate, the only reason I've put you on suspension is because I'm worried sick about you. You're just plain out of control.'

'I know what I'm doing, Jeff.'

'Do you, Kate? I'm sure you've never dealt with treacherous people before. I have. I'm especially concerned about you and Ty Garrison.'

'You might be wrong about him.'

'You think I'm wrong? Is that because you're falling for Garrison? I've done a lot of checking on him. Garrison's got a criminal record. He's spent time in Belle County jail for fighting and disruptive behaviour. That proves what he is!'

Kate made no reply.

'People like him never change. I'm asking you as a personal favour — just stay away from him, at least until all of this is settled.' Jeff stared at her solemnly. 'Even if Garrison is innocent, you're never going to be happy with a man like him. A drifter, that's what he is. He'll stay in Rock Creek a while, then one day he'll just hit the road, wandering off chasing clouds and butterflies. You don't want that kind of a life, Kate. I know that because I know your goals are the same as mine.'

He quickly turned away from her, his habit when he didn't want to hear any more on the subject.

With a choked feeling in her throat, Kate left. In all fairness she couldn't blame Jeff, just herself for defying his orders.

Kate considered making an appeal to Ben, but he had enough to handle with his health problems. She thought now of how much she admired him, how he had supported her when no one else had. She already knew in her heart that this time Ben wouldn't back her up. He would, if for no other reason than concern for her safety, put his stamp of approval on Jeff's decision.

What if the suspension ended in termination? Knowing this was a real possibility, Kate cringed a little. Feeling sombre and defeated, she felt that her career that meant so much to her had fallen around her in ruins.

She would probably leave Rock Creek, but not until she found Charles Kingsley's killer. She would continue working on her own until the murderer was behind bars.

Fast-falling shadows of evening were beginning to gather. Kate walked with slow steps back to her apartment, knowing the long evening would be filled with replays of that muffled voice, that horrible masked face. She was jolted to find Ty waiting for her.

He wore a tan shirt and a rugged suede jacket that spanned his broad shoulders in a tailored fit. Denim jeans and cowboy boots made his legs look long and lean.

'Kate, can I persuade you to go with me tonight? To the annual chili cook-off. A chili-making contest, a tradition here in Rock Creek. The whole county usually shows up. What do you say?'

Jeff's warning words echoed into the stillness. Even though she mustn't trust Ty, she couldn't pass up the opportunity to mingle with the suspects and maybe in doing so, uncover the truth.

'The park's not far. We'll just walk.'

Kate fell into step beside him. Ty guided her toward the festive crowd that overflowed

Rock Creek's park. Lights glowed brilliantly from bulbs draped across trees. About twelve booths, representing tonight's chefs, had set up around a huge space filled with picnic tables where, in the centre blazed a huge bonfire. Just beyond that, music drifted from a cement platform, already crammed with dancers. Encircled by brilliant bulbs draped across poles and trees, they looked like wind-up toys on a stage.

'We'll have to try Swen's chili first,' Ty said. 'Otherwise, he'll be insulted.'

'Glad you could make it tonight, Kate,' Swen said, obviously in a good mood. He stirred the reddish-brown bubbling contents of a large pot as he spoke. 'Mine's an old family recipe handed down from generation to generation. You haven't tasted anything,' he boasted, 'until you've tried this.'

He heaped a generous amount of his chili into their bowls. Kate ate a spoonful and nearly choked.

Ty sampled it and said with pride, 'It's a sure winner.'

'I won last year, but only by a small margin. So don't forget to vote. Early and often,' he called as they wandered off.

'What's his secret ingredient?' Kate asked, eyes watering and her mouth still burning. 'Cayenne pepper?'

'It's not too strong. You're just too weak.' Ty took her bowl from her and finished that off too, all done without a grimace.

'How can you do that?' Kate asked.

'Professional loyalty.' Ty grinned. 'But, just to be fair, we'll have to try some of the others, too. There's Jennie Kingsley. Maybe a lady cook will be more to your liking.'

They strolled toward her booth. Like Swen, she wore a long apron, but hers was marked Rocking C. She swept at the blonde hair that had spilled across her forehead as she said with enthusiasm, 'I've made some cornbread, too.' She added in a lower tone. 'That's the only chance I have of beating Swen.'

Her chili, more to Kate's liking, consisted of a perfect balance of meat, tomatoes, and sauce. After trying several more entries, Kate said finally, 'This is too confusing. I don't think I'll vote.'

'I insist,' Ty said. 'May the best man, or woman win!' His eyes sparkled as they each wrote a name and placed it into the huge, makeshift ballot box.

'Would you look at that swarm of people around Swen's booth,' Ty said. 'I'd better give him a hand.'

After a while, feeling lonely without Ty, Kate spotted Mary Ellen seated on a park bench away from the others. Gold barrettes clipped the sides of hair that matched the streaks of light shimmering through it. The style of her dress, soft blue with a flowing skirt, made her look like a young girl.

Kate approached her, trying hard to catch the party spirit. 'Who's going to win?'

'Swen,' she said. 'He always does. But last year he only beat Uncle Charles by twelve votes.' Mary Ellen's wan smile added to her girlish look. 'You should have heard him raging. He claimed that Swen had cheated, that his ranch hands had voted more than once.'

'What's the prize?' Kate asked lightly. 'Is it worth an under-the-table deal?'

'Every merchant donates a gift,' Mary Ellen said. 'The Tumbleweed Café gives the winner a free meal.'

'I should have set up my own stand.'

'Not much at stake, but enough for a battle between Swen and my uncle. I smile about it, but it's not funny the way they hated each other.' Mary Ellen fell silent, her gaze skimming the crowd.

'Are you waiting for someone?'

'Jake Pierson, who I work with at the museum. He said he'd be here tonight,' Mary Ellen added, almost blushing. 'He told me to save my first dance for him.'

'He knows so much about Wyoming history. This must be a great interest of yours, too.'

'Not really. I only volunteer to help him out. I actually don't understand why people get so caught up in the past. That's what Uncle Charles always did. Shouldn't people live for now, think more about today than yesterday?'

'Yesterday keeps coming back in different forms,' Kate remarked. Mary Ellen's reaction, an apparent shrinking away, surprised Kate. She hadn't intended her offhand comment to spark unpleasant memories. Kate cast her a quick glance. Her words must have caused Mary Ellen to think of her own past, of the boy she had lost so long ago that had been the love of her life. Hard, Kate thought, to let go and move on, but this was what Mary Ellen was attempting to do. That's why she had shown up here tonight.

'Isn't that him now?' Kate asked.

Jake Pierson once again brought to Kate's mind images of Buffalo Bill Cody, the fringed jacket he wore, the way his longish hair was pulled back and knotted with a buckskin tie. His eyes lit up when they fell upon Mary Ellen. 'Ready for that dance?'

'Excuse us,' Mary Ellen said politely, rising and taking his offered hand.

Mary Ellen had placed herself away from the others, not wanting to be the centre of attention. Now all eyes seemed fastened on the two as they made their way through the crowd and a little awkwardly, like teenagers at a first dance, joined the whirling couples. Kate idly watched as they attempted to keep up with the too-fast music, then her gaze shifted to the trees along the north side of the platform. The glint of pale blond hair, illuminated the low-hanging bulbs, almost brought a gasp to her lips.

Slim Barton stood huddling from the chill, thin shoulders hunched, eyes burning as he stared at Mary Ellen. Burning with what: jealousy? One fact became clear, Slim Barton was either very close to Mary Ellen or else he wanted to be.

Kate glanced back at Mary Ellen just in time to see her look towards Barton, then turn her head quickly away, as if pretending not to see him. Riff-raff, low-life; Charles Kingsley's words described Barton perfectly. The thought struck Kate with great force: Slim Barton could be Mary Ellen's old boyfriend, the one her uncle had refused to let her marry. Astounded, Kate stared at him, noticing the way his bold, defiant eyes remained locked on Mary Ellen. He was probably about two or three years older than her and that meant that Barton and Mary Ellen could have met years ago when he was around eighteen and she sixteen. If so, Kate could sympathize with Charles Kingsley's stand on the matter. In his place, she would have done exactly as he had, tried any way he could to protect Mary Ellen from a man like him.

All assumption, Kate reminded herself, leaning back against the bench; after all, Mary Ellen was gazing up at Pierson as if no other man existed. Kate couldn't base a whole theory on a stranger who just happened to find Mary Ellen attractive. Yet suddenly, it seemed very important to her to find out whom Mary Ellen had loved and probably still did. If he had come back to Rock Creek, expecting that Mary Ellen would inherit a fortune from her uncle, this might make a big difference to her investigation into Kingsley's death.

The music stopped. The bandleader announced a short intermission. The couples left the floor, mingling with the swarm of people still eating. Kate looked for Slim Barton, but he had disappeared into the crowd.

Ty had left Swen's booth. As she rose to search for him she spotted Lem, still in uniform, cutting across the park. He stopped at Swen's booth for some chili and ambled on. Lem had been in Rock Creek all his life. If anyone would know the name of Mary Ellen's old boyfriend, it would be him.

He took a seat close to Jennie's stand. Hal Barkley, wearing a long apron like Jennie's, dipped large helpings of chili into paper bowls. Jennie, with pleasant talk and banter, stood beside him offering cornbread.

'Didn't think you'd be here.' Kate slipped into the seat across from Lem.

'Doing my duty,' Lem told her. He sampled Swen's chili, but didn't take a second spoonful, just stirred the thick soup. 'To tell you the truth,' he said in a confidential tone, 'this stuff gives me heartburn.'

Kate laughed.

'We found the car,' Lem said. 'It belonged to Hal Barkley, who claims someone hotwired it and stole it from his property. It had been dumped in some pasture on the road to Downing. The boys went over it, and you can guess the results.'

'The usual dead end. Lem, did you ever meet Mary Ellen's boyfriend, the one Mr Kingsley wouldn't let her marry?'

The question or the abrupt change of subject took him by surprise. 'Why do you ask that?'

'I think it may be important.'

'That was a long time ago.' Lem cautiously took another taste of Swen's chili and gave a shuddering headshake. 'Kingsley was always berating and condemning the boy to everyone who would listen. But he didn't use any name that I recall beyond punk, rascal, or deadbeat.'

'Who would know him?'

'From what I hear Mary Ellen and he did a lot of sneaking around. Maybe no one.'

'Someone will,' Kate declared. 'I need to locate Mary Ellen's old boyfriend. One way or another, I'm going to find him.'

A rush of people had converged upon Jennie's stand. One brushing close to Kate, caused her to look up, right into Slim Barton's cold eyes. Slim stood just behind Jake Pierson, who was saying affably to Jennie, 'I hear your chili is making a big hit tonight.'

Kate glanced over her shoulder and skimmed the crowd for Mary Ellen. She found her just beyond Swen's booth, talking to Ty. They both looked very serious.

'Garrison could be your man,' Lem said, pointing his spoon in the direction Kate was looking. 'He was working for Swen at about that time and would be the right age.'

'But her boyfriend was employed by

Kingsley.'

'You have no idea how many hands those two ranches employ. So many extras are hired during branding and roundup even the employers have trouble recognizing them. Often, when offered higher wages the men jumped ship and went to the rival ranch, which was a bone of contention between them.' Lem leaned closer to her, his voice dropping an octave lower. 'The Double S and the Rocking C were really locking horns at the time. Swen probably sent Garrison to court Mary Ellen.'

'Why?'

'To torment Kingsley, why else? That's the game the two men played.'

Kate looked toward Ty again. This time her gaze met his, and both he and Mary Ellen started toward them.

'Been looking all over for you,' Ty said. 'Thought you had given me the slip and went home. You ready to dance?'

The music had started again. Ty and Kate stopped beside the bonfire for a while, then joined the dancers. Bright stars, Ty smiling down at her: tonight could have been perfect. The slow tune soon changed to a fast beat. Kate, spinning and laughing, momentarily forgot Lem's words. They ended their dance breathless. During the next, 'The

Waltz of the Wind,' Kate thought of Jeff. She felt relief that he wasn't here to see her dancing with Ty, to see the way Ty's eyes shone when they looked into hers.

An important-looking man who reminded her of Ben came up on stage. He gestured to the band, who stopped playing, and took the microphone from the stand. 'Ladies and gentlemen, we have our vote!'

Everyone clapped.

'The winner of the Rock Creek chili cook-off is. . . . Wait, first I want all the contestants to join me on stage.'

Representatives from the twelve booths complied; Swen, stopping to remove his apron and put on his Stetson. He looked very tall and strong standing next to Jennie.

'The winner tonight — would you believe this — we have a winner by only one vote! A near tie: Jennie Kingsley, 78; Sam Swen, 77.'

Amid the uproar of applause, Swen stepped closer to the microphone. He slanted a look back at the beaming Jennie, and said with a smile, 'Maybe I had better demand a recount.'

'Votes were counted twice,' the master of ceremonies assured him.

'Could be an error,' Swen declared.

'You're such an old spoilsport,' Jennie

spoke up, also with laughter in her voice. 'I guess I'll have to let you share the crown with me.'

'No, lady.' Swen took off his hat. 'I'll just concede.'

More applause.

'It's time Swen faced the truth,' Ty called out merrily. 'There's a new cook in town.'

'There's always next year,' Swen returned, then said to Jennie, 'If this chili is better than mine, then I want to try some.'

They left the platform together, Ty and Kate trailing after them to Jennie's booth. Jennie put a modest amount of chili into a bowl and watched Swen as he sampled it.

'What do you think?'

'I know when I've been beaten,' Swen said, but the look in his eyes was warm and admiring.

Ty's hand slipped around Kate's as they walked back towards her apartment, basking in the after-effects of the outcome that hinted at a kind of truce between the two rival ranches. When they reached the door Ty said, 'Poor Swen, to lose by so slight a margin.' He gave Kate an amused, sideways glance. 'You must have cast the deciding vote. Tell me, which one did you vote for?'

'For Swen,' Kate confessed, 'but I don't know why.'

Ty smiled. 'I do. I'm loyal to Swen, and you're loyal to me.' Ty drew her into his arms and kissed her. In a soft, gentle voice, he said, 'Good night, darling. I'll call you soon.'

CHAPTER 11

Kate sat by the mirror, brushing dark curls, seeing a new glow in her eyes as she thought of Ty's kiss and of his arms around her. Even the ringing of the phone, which often annoyed her, sounded happy. Ty had told her he'd call soon, hadn't he? Smiling, Kate lifted the receiver in anticipation.

The muffled words jolted her. 'You've had your last warning. If you don't quit poking your nose where it doesn't belong, you're going to end up just like Kingsley. Dead.'

A click sounded, followed by a dial tone. Kate stared at the black receiver, repulsed by it, as if it had turned into some deadly snake. The caller had disguised his voice, but she was convinced he was the same man who had set a trap for her this afternoon.

'. . . your last warning.' the exact words Swen had spoken the day he had found her stranded along the road on the way back from Pauley's Auction Barn.

Kate set to work at once, calling close neighbours to the Rocking C. They all remembered that Mary Ellen had an early tragic love encounter, remembered that she was barely sixteen at the time and was devastated when the boy left town, but no one could recall ever hearing his name. Determined to find him, Kate decided to confront Mary Ellen with the question.

Mary Ellen, looking scared and alone, much as she had when Kate had first seen her, opened the door a crack. 'If you're looking for Jennie,' she said, 'she's not here.'

'It's you I want to see. May I come in?'

Reluctantly Mary Ellen stepped aside. The study looked different today washed in sunlight streaming in from the wide-open curtains. Despite the brightness, the polished cases filled with Wild West displays, Kate thought only of Charles Kingsley lying dead on the floor near his desk.

Mary Ellen sank down in her uncle's chair. Kate found her gaze roaming as it always did when she entered this room to the invitation to Tom Horn's hanging.

'Why do you want to talk to me?'

Kate didn't answer her question, instead she asked, 'Where did Jennie go?'

'Business, or so she said.'

The bitterness in Mary Ellen's tone discredited any reference to business. 'She didn't mention where she were going?'

'No, she barely talks to me. I hear rumours that she's always run around with a lot of men. I don't think my uncle should have . . . married her.' Mary Ellen's large eyes lifted to Kate's. 'You know what I told you about her and Swen?'

'I heard they dated at one time, but that was back in the past.'

'They've never stopped seeing each other.'

'You know that for a fact? Maybe they are just long-time friends.'

'They sneak around,' Mary Ellen said dully, 'I've seen them.'

Kate turned away from the girl, stepping closer to the framed invitation and looking at it absently as she talked. 'I understand you had a boyfriend that your uncle didn't approve of. I need to know his name.' Kate's gaze flickered to Mary Ellen, taking note of her pale, stricken face. She couldn't have looked more stunned if Kate had struck her a hard, physical blow.

'Why is that important? I'm twenty-eight years old. I haven't lain eyes on him for over twelve years.'

'Mary Ellen, I think he may have come back here. He tried to rob your uncle once.

He might have attempted the same thing again.'

'That was so many years ago. He just got drunk one night, a boyish act. Now he's a man. He wouldn't still be doing things like that.'

'If you haven't seen him for so long,' Kate asked, "how do you know? He could have turned into an alcoholic and a big time thief as well. Besides that, he would bear a grudge against your uncle, which might explain the stone placed under his head.'

Mary Ellen, too upset for more denials, made no reply.

'Tell me his name. I'll check him out and if I find he was somewhere else when the crime was committed, that will be the end of it.'

Kate had expected Mary Ellen to refuse to cooperate, but after a long, heavy silence, she said, 'His name is David Glenwood Colbert. After David left here, he went to Denver. I never saw him again. He didn't even write or try to call me.'

The moment Kate returned to her apartment, she phoned the sheriff's office. Luckily Lem answered. 'I need for you to run a check on a David Glenwood Colbert. His middle name was probably his mother's maiden name so it should be no problem sorting him out from other Colberts. This is very important, Lem, can you do it right away?'

'I'll get back to you as soon as possible.'

Glad that she merited Lem's continual support, Kate waited impatiently by the phone. When it finally rang again, she grabbed the receiver anxiously.

'Kate, nothing's turned up on any man by that name. No criminal record.'

'I knew Kingsley hadn't brought charges against him, but I thought he was the type to have eventually built up a rap sheet. Were you able to trace him through his social security number?'

'No one's listed by that name. He either died before he got a social security number, or he's got himself an alias.'

Or Mary Ellen had simply made up a name because she didn't want to reveal his real one. Another dead end, unless Kate had been on the right track and she had seen Mary Ellen's boyfriend face to face at last night's cook-off. 'Have you found out anything else about Slim Barton?'

'His real name's Dean Barton, but everyone knows him as Slim. He owns his own ranch, the Bar 8, just south of here near the Colorado border.'

'Swen says he's buying up land. How big

is his operation?'

'Very small. He doesn't have enough acreage to run too many head of cattle.'

'Do you know the brand he uses?'

'Sure. A simple bar and an eight.'

'Thanks, Lem.'

After she hung up the phone, Kate sketched Kingsley's brand on a notepad, then drew an eight with a bar beneath it. By adding a couple of loops, the Rocking C without any problem at all could be transformed into an eight. In the same way Swen's Double S could be changed into Barton's brand. Perhaps Barton had for many years been stealing from both ranches. He had probably set up his operation with the Bar 8 name for exactly this purpose.

No wonder she hadn't been able to trace the sales. Slim Barton had stolen from both ranches with impunity, certain one would blame the other. He had altered both brands to the Bar 8 before they were consigned. Since Slim Barton was a rancher himself, no one would even be suspicious.

Kate began calling all of the area's livestock auctions telling them she was interested in purchasing Bar 8 cattle from Slim Barton. She went through the entire list, the results being the same: he had dealt with none of them.

She extended her search into Colorado. Sheffield's Cattle Trade was located close to Barton's ranch, just over the state line. The clerk connected her to the boss.

'I'm Kate Jepp from the Belle County sheriff's department and I need some information. Have you sold cattle for Charles Kingsley or for Sam Swen?'

She remained on hold for a long time.

'We have made no sales for either of them.'

'What about Slim Barton?'

'Yes, he sells here occasionally.'

'Does he have a consignment for your next auction?'

'Not unless he's just brought them in. The auction is tomorrow.'

'Would you be able to fax me some records concerning his total sales for the past two years?' Kate gave him her fax number, replaced the phone and waited. When the fax came through, she scanned the figures. Just as he had said, the Bar 8 sales wcre infrequent and limited as would be expected for an operation of his size.

Then what had Slim Barton done with the load of Herefords stolen from the Rocking C Sunday night? Either he had taken them to his ranch . . . or to Pauley's, the only livestock auction in the area that she hadn't just called.

Dread filled her at the prospect of confronting Pauley again. During their last ugly encounter, she had suspected him of working with the rustlers for a cut of the profit. Yet she could be wrong. He might simply resist the idea of disclosing information concerning his two major consigners, Kingsley and Swen, but he might be willing to talk about Barton.

The long stretch of isolated road to Downing gave her time to think. Kate reached the rough gully where the Landcruiser had lost a wheel. She thought of the way Sam Swen had suddenly appeared along the isolated road and had stopped supposedly to help her. The same doubt and fear rose in her now as then. The loosened lug nuts, Swen's timely arrival, could have been planned in advance, the same way the Chevy wreck had been set up. She might have handed over the incriminating evidence to Swen himself, concealed behind cowboy hat and ski mask.

Jeff had maintained Swen's guilt from the beginning: Swen the brains behind the den of rustlers, the man who had ordered Kingsley's death if he hadn't pulled the trigger himself. Yet only one fact was certain to Kate: more than one person could be playing a major role in this highly successful swindle. Nor could she just assume Slim

Barton was the head man, when it was just as likely he was taking orders from someone higher up.

Relieved to have the deserted miles behind her, Kate pulled into the near-empty lot beside Pauley's Auction Barn. A heavy-set man in overalls stood near the cattle pens. 'Do you work here?'

'Sure do,' he said, spitting out tobacco.

'Has Slim Barton consigned any cattle for tomorrow's auction?'

'Usually does. Fact is, he told me yesterday he planned to sell at least a dozen head of prime Herefords. Just hasn't brought them in yet.'

'Do you accept them so late?'

'Sure do. Something must have happened, though. Slim always gets his lot in early. If you're interested, Pauley could make a call for you and check on his consignment.'

Inside, met with silence and empty bleachers, Kate's wariness increased. She started down the dim, circular corridor leading to Pauley's office, there she paused and drew a deep breath, trying to prepare herself for another unpleasant encounter with the rude owner.

A cheery voice called out, 'Hi.' A woman's face, topped with coppery hair piled high and clipped with rhinestone barrettes, appeared above the partition. She looked to be around forty, about the same age as Pauley.

'You must be Pauley's wife,' Kate said in a friendly manner.

'Yes, I'm Ruth. Hank's around here somewhere. I can find him if you like.'

'Maybe you can help me.' Kate took out the ID she had failed to turn in with her badge and gun. The woman glanced at the photo, then at her, smiling pleasantly. What a break. Hank Pauley hadn't mentioned Kate's last visit to his wife.

'I spoke to Mr Pauley earlier about obtaining some sales records — just a routine check for an investigation I'm doing.'

'What records do you need? I can pull them up for you on the computer in a jiffy.'

The moment Kate told her, with quick movements of fingers, nails painted to match her hair, she called up Sam Swen's account. His steady sales showed no inconsistencies. Kingsley's as well revealed nothing out of the ordinary.

'How about Slim Barton's Bar 8?'

Kate couldn't quite believe the huge amount of business Barton had been doing with Pauley's Auction over the past few months. 'What I'll need are the figures for the year.'

Ruth pressed a few keys, generating a spreadsheet. Kate skimmed the great number of sales, realizing that he'd sold more beef than Swen and Kingsley combined, much more than his small ranch could possibly support.

'I can make you a print-out of this,' Ruth offered.

'If it's not too much trouble. Could you include the Rocking C and the Double S as well?'

The printer clicked and whirred. They waited as it spilled out pages. 'There you go, Miss Jepp.'

As Ruth handed over the run-off copy, footsteps sounded in the hallway just outside the office. Kate stuffed the papers in her purse and swung around, face to face with Hank Pauley.

He stopped short. 'So you're back again?' he growled. 'Didn't I make it clear enough last time?'

Ruth looked from one to the other of them, bewildered by her husband's hostile reaction. Pauley's gaze slid from his wife to the computer screen still displaying Swen's records.

Kate tensed.

'Going behind my back! I ought to throw you out of here!'

'Hank, what's wrong?' Ruth asked. 'This girl is from the sheriff's office.'

'Ben didn't send her, you can count on that. Meddling, that's what she's doing.' He glared at Kate. 'You and I need to talk.'

He ushered Kate ahead of him through the door. His tight grip caused ripples of pain to shoot through her recently injured arm. He didn't let go of her until they had reached the centre corridor.

Last time he had been angry, now he was livid. The way his eyes glittered made Kate half-afraid of him.

'Hand over those papers she gave you.'

Kate made no move to comply.

Pauley took a step closer to her as if he planned to yank away her purse and take them by force.

'Hank!' Ruth's call stopped him. She reached them in seconds. Fingers with their coppery nails clamped over his wrist. 'Hank, what's wrong with you?'

To Kate's surprise, Ruth's words calmed him. He dropped his hands to his sides and said almost docilely, 'I have instructions. Swen told me straight out, he doesn't want any of his records released without a court order.'

'I'm not working for the Kingsleys,' Kate told him. 'The information your wife gave me will be confidential.'

'I've always supported Swen.' Pauley looked away, speaking as if he hadn't even heard her. When his eyes settled again on Kate, he tried to change the implication of his words. 'Kingsley was flat out crazy making all those accusations against him.'

'If Swen's innocent, he has nothing to fear from me.'

'You'd better leave now,' Ruth cut in. She tugged on Pauley's arm, saying soothingly, 'Don't worry, Hank. I'll call Swen. I'll explain.'

The glitter in Pauley's eyes returned. His words, almost a yell, rang out harsh and accusatory, 'You don't know what you've done, do you? You've just ruined everything!'

With Pauley's last statement replaying in her mind, Kate pulled on to the highway. Kate had ruined everything: what on earth could Pauley mean by that? Was he referring to her being on the trail of Barton and her making the connection between the Bar 8 and Sam Swen?

The only way she could prove Barton was involved was to find the stolen cattle which, according to her calculations, must still be at the Bar 8 Ranch. But it would take nerve to go out there alone, knowing as she did, that right now Pauley would be on the phone to Swen.

Still, she had a time advantage. With Swen and his crew in Rock Creek, she would be able to reach the Bar 8 at least an hour before them. Pauley might, however, alert Slim Barton, but she wouldn't consider that now. She would think only about grasping what was beginning to look like her last opportunity.

Slim Barton's ranch, amid a rocky hillside, couldn't be compared to the vast, rich spreads of either Swen or Kingsley. It consisted of a run-down wood-frame house, an ancient barn with a sagging roof and a few dilapidated outbuildings. To Kate's disappointment no cattle milled inside the corral or grazed in the grassland beyond it. As if unable to believe it, she drove around the Bar 8 pastureland again. He must have wised up, had already rebranded the stolen cattle and moved them out.

She had driven out here for nothing. Still, it couldn't hurt to take a look around. A distance away from the house, she edged her Landcruiser into a thick grove of pine trees. She had to cross an open field on foot.

No one appeared to be anywhere around. Kate moved quickly but cautiously, like a soldier crossing into enemy territory. She slipped into the barn where she drew her first deep breath since she had trespassed on Barton's land.

Overhead, light streamed through gaps in the sagging roof, casting hazy streaks into the dimness. A strong odour of damp hay hung around her, mingling with scents of fuel and grease.

Kate moved towards an assortment of tools scattered on a workbench against the back wall. She stopped to examine a row of branding irons hung from pegs. Because the area, generally used to store equipment, was totally empty, Kate assumed she had found the secret workplace where Barton changed the stolen Hereford's brands to his.

As Kate turned back to look for cattle restraints, she drew in her breath. Her heart seemed to jolt to a stop. Ty stood in the centre of the barn. The indirect glow from the open doors behind him made him look cold and sinister.

No look of surprise crossed his face. Clearly he knew she would be here. They must all work together, never out of contact, like some deadly army patrol. Pauley must have called Ty, just as he had called Swen that day her Landcruiser had crashed, just as Ty had called Swen telling him about the evidence she had found in the canyon.

Swen, Ty, and Pauley — but Slim Barton could be included, too. Unless no one had called Ty, unless he often worked here, unless he rather than Swen headed the operation

Fear gripped her. 'What are you doing here?' she asked hollowly.

'No, you tell me what you're doing here.'

'I'm checking out a theory of mine. I've been thinking that Slim Barton may be Mary Ellen's old boyfriend. She had one years ago, when she was sixteen or so, but Mr Kingsley wouldn't allow her to marry him.'

Kate thought she noted some change in Ty, a slight narrowing of his eyes, a tightening of his lips. She hurried on, 'He was a thief to begin with. He might be targeting the Kingsley ranch in order to settle an old score.'

Ty responded with a soft-spoken question. 'After all these years?'

'Resentment often grows deeper with time. You told me you were working for Swen then. Didn't you ever run across this boy or hear his name mentioned?'

'I know nothing about Mary Ellen's personal life.' Ty took a step closer. 'I got a call from Pauley. He saw you start out this way and thought you might be heading for trouble.'

'Then he . . . works with Swen, too?'

His rugged features showed no change this time, just remained hard and unreadable. 'Of course.'

Kate thought with sinking heart about that day Ty and she had ridden their horses into the canyon. What if his interest had not been in her, but in saving Swen?

'Kate, you're getting deeper and deeper into danger. You must leave here at once. From now on you must stay completely out of this.'

'I can't.'

'If you would only let us handle this. Pauley has been working directly with Swen. We've told him about the microchips we've embedded into our cattle, and he's been waiting for them to show up. So far, none have. But once they do, Swen will be cleared for good.' A frown cut between his eyes. 'Or so we thought. But now it looks as if this isn't going to happen.'

'Why not? Barton would have no way of knowing about the chips.'

'Barton must have seen you at the auction and you scared him off. At least that's what Pauley believes. And it is beginning to look as if he's right, that Barton isn't going to consign any more Herefords to Pauley's auction.'

'What has he done with the cattle he took the other night, then?' Kate asked. 'They're not here.'

'I'd say he sold them to a private individual. Or transported them to the ranch of some friend. At any rate, it's clear he's decided to lay low.'

Kate stared at him. If she believed Ty, then instead of solving the case, she had only been interfering. She had just kept Swen and Ty from catching Slim Barton. She had bungled, made another blunder that Jeff could add to his ever-growing list.

'Don't look so worried, Kate. We're not beaten yet,' Ty said. 'We'll think of some other way. . . .'

Ty's words were stopped by the sound of an engine. He went to the entrance, flattened himself against the barn door, then ventured a look out.

Kate, followed suit, taking up a post on the other side of the doorway. An old truck rattled along, pulling to a jerky stop beside the house. Shaggy lengths of pale blond hair caught the wind as Slim Barton got out. He seemed alert to some hidden danger. He remained with one hand on the open truck door as he looked around.

'No, Ty.' Kate caught Ty's arm, but he effortlessly freed her grasp.

'Stay in here,' Ty said. He stepped outside, calling, 'Barton!'

Slim Barton's wiry form stiffened. Ty strode toward him. Kate, afraid of what might happen, remained immobile for a few seconds, then quickly followed.

'You got scared, didn't you, when you realized Swen and Pauley were on to you. So you disposed of the last load of stolen Herefords somewhere else.'

'What are you talking about?'

'The fact that you're too late. One of Swen's microchips was found on cattle you consigned to Pauley's. That's why I'm here now.'

What was Ty thinking? No microchips had been found. Ty must be desperate believing a sly man like Barton would fall for anything like this.

'That's nonsense,' Barton snapped.

Ty continued with his bluff, saying convincingly, 'I brought the law with me.' He nodded toward Kate. 'You can explain to her how our cattle ended up with your brand.'

Barton didn't answer, didn't move. His words were steady as he said to Kate, 'If this happened, if anything like that was found, I've been set up.'

'Don't even try it. Your partner has already pointed a finger at you.'

Another story Ty had just made up. Kate could do nothing else but play along. 'I'm going to ask you to accompany us back to Rock Creek.'

'I'm not going anywhere. Garrison is the one behind this. He's rigged this all up so he won't be blamed himself.'

Ty took a threatening step closer, his hands clenching into fists. Kate drew in her breath. Surely Ty didn't intend to attack Slim in the same way he had attacked Kingsley's foreman when he had come to Swen's ranch.

'I know just how you robbed from both ranches,' Ty said evenly. 'I'd say it's all over now, all over . . . but the hanging.'

Ty's last words proved too much for Slim Barton. In panic, with the speed of a cat, Barton swung around, clawing and crawling his way back into the truck. Kate couldn't see him. He must be pressed flat against the front seat. She caught no movement until the barrel of a rifle poked out the window.

'Look out, Ty!'

She expected Ty to duck for cover, instead he lunged forward. He caught the gun barrel, wrested it away from Barton, and at the same time pulled open the door. As if Slim Barton were weightless, Ty jerked him from the cab and sent him sprawling across the ground.

'I'll keep an eye on him,' Ty said, lifting Slim Barton's gun and training it on him, 'You go call the sheriff's office.'

'I want to talk to you,' Jeff said, looking big and solid in his uniform.

Kate stepped into his office, and he firmly closed the door, shutting out the clamour from the next room.

'I can't believe this!' he raged. 'You don't have a scrap of evidence against this man!'

Kate made no reply.

'You told him some stupid lies you just pulled out of the air. Why? Why on earth did you do that?'

Kate started to say that she hadn't lied to him, but changed her words. 'We thought he might confess.'

'Well, he didn't. All you've got on him is the fact that he pulled a gun on you. But it was you and Garrison on his land, harassing him! Moreover, he didn't even get off a shot. I'm booking him, all right, but he'll be out of here in nothing flat.'

Jeff stared at her in that uncompromising way she so despised.

'Is that all?'

'No, there's that and so much more!' His voice had become hard and brittle. 'What did you plan to do? Make a citizen's arrest? Putting you on suspension didn't stop you. You're just plain out of control!'

Kate's lack of reply fueled Jeff's anger. 'Did this ever occur to you: instead of Swen embedding microchips in his own cattle, he might be planting them into ones bearing Slim Barton's brand to get himself off the hook.'

'Or it could be we've caught the real rustler.'

Jeff seemed not to hear her. 'Look at it this way. All along Swen's been tormenting Kingsley by stealing from his herd. Now that Kingsley's dead, so is his grudge against the Rocking C.' Jeff paused, sucking in his breath. 'Everyone believes Swen's guilty because of that lawsuit. Now he wants his name cleared. And what better way than to set up some poor rancher like Barton?'

'I think you're wrong about Swen, Jeff.'

'It doesn't matter what you think.' He turned away. 'Your position here is in serious jeopardy now, I want you to know that.'

'There's things more important to me than this job,' Kate answered and left the sheriff's office without looking back.

CHAPTER 12

Totally defeated, Kate spent a dreary evening in her apartment sorting through clues and coming up with absolutely nothing. She slept on the sofa, forms and notes stacked around her. Early the next morning she was jarred awake by the insistent ringing of her phone.

'Kate, Swen here.' Normally his words were weighted with burden and responsibility, but not this morning. 'I've just talked to Ben at the hospital.' Swen stopped for a moment, chuckling. 'Told the old boy that next election I was of a mind to vote for you instead of him.'

'How's Ben doing?'

'He'll be fine,' Swen replied, 'if you can keep him away from the pastries.' The merriment faded from his voice. 'Kate, I've got some good news for you. I've heard from Sheffield's Cattle Trade. My little plan hit pay dirt. Sheffield's found two of my chips

in the cattle Slim Barton consigned yesterday afternoon. Barton's caught red-handed.
Jeff's at the sheriff's office taking Barton's
statement now, so you'll probably want to
be on hand.' Swen chuckled again. 'Didn't
think you would want to miss out on all the
fun.'

Inside the sheriff's office Jeff and Lem
were questioning Slim Barton. Jeff glanced
up as Kate entered, his expression bearing
no hint of the gruff, 'what are you doing
here?' she had expected.

Barton, scared and shaken, slumped
against the table. His face, drained of colour, blended with the shaggy strands of pale
hair. 'They're trying to pin Kingsley's
murder on me,' he said desperately.

'You had motive,' Lem cut in, his tone
slow and certain. 'All along you've been
stealing from both ranches, pitting one
against the other. Charles Kingsley found
you out. That Monday night he caught you
on his land, dragged you into his study and
confronted you. He intended to call us, to
hold you at gunpoint until we arrived. You
managed to get his revolver away from him
and used it to shoot him. You put that stone
under Kingsley's head to lead us off track,
to make his murder look like revenge. You
knew we wouldn't have to look far, only

down the road to find an enemy.'

'I'm no killer!'

'Then how do you explain shooting me?' Kate asked.

'That bullet hit right where I was aiming, for your shoulder not for your heart. I'm a crack shot. Ask anyone.' Barton's angry eyes met hers. 'I just meant to scare you away. If I'd wanted you dead, you wouldn't be standing here right now.'

Barton stopped short, realizing what he had said amounted to a confession concerning the rustling charge.

'Who are you working with?' Kate demanded.

'I'm not saying another word. I need a lawyer.'

'That you do,' Lem replied, rising and escorting Barton towards the phone in the outer office.

'Nothing connects me with the old man's death!' he shouted back at Kate. 'I was just trying to make ends meet. You might get me for selling a little beef on the side, but never for murder.'

'I'd say you're lucky the way things turned out,' Jeff said after they had left. 'The way you handled this, it could have ended in disaster. Your going out and confronting Barton without any proof was just plain reckless.'

Kate had never intended that to happen: Ty had done that on his own. She made no comment, just asked, 'What about my job? Do I still have one?'

'That's not up to me; that's Ben's decision. You broke the rules and you know what a stickler he is for rules.'

Kate started for the door. 'Barton's right, you know. We'll never be able to charge him with Kingsley's murder. It will remain unsolved.'

'Not a chance.' Jeff smiled, radiating a high good spirit. 'The county attorney will indict him for everything. This case is closed.'

Jeff might be satisfied that Slim Barton had been working alone rustling cattle from both Kingsley and Swen, but Kate had deep misgivings. If Kingsley had uncovered the true cattle rustler and confronted him, the broken glass on the door and the placement of the stone just didn't follow. She still maintained that someone had come into the study to steal while Kingsley was safely out of the way.

The stone remained in Kate's mind as it had from the first, a sign of bitter hatred. It had to have been placed by someone who knew about the feud between Swen and

Kingsley and about the legend of Tom Horn, who had set beneath his victim's heads what Swen referred to as a 'stone of vengeance'.

Slim Barton was no history buff. She doubted he would ever think of setting up Swen in this way.

For a while Kate drove around aimlessly, then found herself heading for the Kingsley ranch.

'Jennie. It's Kate.' No one answered, still Kate pushed open the door whose shattered glass had finally been replaced. Jennie sat behind Kingsley's desk, slumped in his big leather chair, a place that seemed to give her comfort. She huddled, arms pressing a heavy, turquoise-coloured jacket close around her as if attempting to ward off a terrible chill.

Jennie stared straight ahead, as if at nothing. Kate watched her silently until Jennie became aware of her presence and looked up.

'Have you heard about Slim Barton's arrest?'

'Yes, Swen called me.' Jennie's usually smiling lips tightened into a drawn line, making her look much older than her years. 'It's all over,' she said solemnly. 'But it will never be over.' Tears brimmed in her eyes.

'Charles is gone, and what am I ever going to do without him?'

'You'll carry on,' Kate said encouragingly. 'Just like Mr Kingsley would have done.'

'Mary Ellen is upstairs in her room. Someone should let her know. She's going to be leaving today, I think.' Jennie sank even deeper in her chair, as if the task of telling Mary Ellen about the crime was too much for her.

'I'll talk to Mary Ellen if you want me to.'

'Would you, Kate?'

Not comfortable with leaving Jennie alone, Kate decided to remain a while. She walked uneasily around the office and drew to a stop in front of the invitation to Tom Horn's hanging. From the first Kate had suspected this unusual collector's relic had been a catalyst for the crime, the key to Kingsley's death.

For a long time she stared at it, wondering how it fit in. At first she thought her eyes were playing tricks on her. The invitation seemed to sit just a shade out of line in the frame, as if it had shifted slightly to the right. Most people wouldn't even notice the barely perceptible difference, but Kate's trained eyes saw every detail. Moreover, the frame itself, which had been hanging crooked, was now perfectly aligned. Without doubt, someone had tampered ever so minutely with both the inside and the outside of the document. Kate leaned closer, noticing yet another change: the paper looked in perfect condition. Too perfect. She gave a little start of surprise. The tiny crease she had noticed in the far left corner had totally disappeared.

Aware of Jennie's soft sobbing from behind her, Kate began to read the flowing, ink-penned letter.

'You are requested to be present at the legal execution of Tom Horn.' She skimmed every line, her gaze locking on the word SHERIFF at the end. The tiny inkblot just above the 'I' in this word was gone. Kate drew in her breath. The original invitation had been replaced with an almost identical forgery!

She whirled to tell this to Jennie. At the same time Jennie, startled, swivelled in the chair to face her. As she did, she released her hold on her jacket and it fell open. Around Jennie's neck hung a necklace. Kate stared at the black background where red and blue beads formed an unusual geometric design — Sioux — a perfect match to the earring found in the truck that had crashed into her squad car.

Kate stared at Jennie aghast, not seeing tears, but instead imagining a triumphant smile. For a moment she felt deep shock. Kate had helped convince Jeff that Swen wasn't involved, but what if she had been wrong? If Swen and Jennie had been working together to set all of this up, they now controlled two of Wyoming's largest spreads.

'What's wrong, Kate?'

Kate stared at her, attempting to deal with these chilling thoughts and suddenly dismissing them as having no logic: Jennie would not wear the very necklace that matched the earring she would surely know she had lost the night of the crash.

Kate turned quickly away. 'I'm going up to tell Mary Ellen now.'

Kate climbed the curving, wooden stairway to the second storey, her hasty steps causing a creaking in the floorboards. She reached Mary Ellen's door, tapping anxiously. When no one answered, she opened it a crack. 'Mary Ellen?'

Mary Ellen had already started to pack. On the bed in front of the near-empty closet a large canvas suitcase gaped open. On top of a neat row of clothes lay a curling iron, a package wrapped in brown paper and several plastic bags. Mary Ellen must be in another part of the house, taking care of some unfinished task.

Kate skimmed the room where Mary Ellen had spent most of her life. Rows of leather-bound books set in a case beside the bed, classic romantic novels, *The Great Gatsby, Wuthering Heights.* She had been emptying drawers, clutter set in little stacks on the dresser. Nothing suggested a life other than the ranch except for the small, heart-shaped picture frame that lay face-down. Kate knew before she lifted the picture that it would be a photograph of Mary Ellen's one true love, the boy Kingsley had chased away. She wondered if it would turn out to be Slim Barton. Kate reached for the picture.

Struck with a horrible thought, Kate felt suddenly reluctant to turn it over. In the silence she recalled Jeff's words, how Kingsley had once filed a restraining order against Ty. She had thought at the time that Ty had merely been trespassing on Kingsley's land, but now it occurred to her that he, not Slim, could have been Mary Ellen's long-lost boyfriend.

Kate hesitated. If she lifted the frame, would she see a younger version of Slim Barton, or Ty as he had looked when he had worked for Swen many years ago? Carefully she raised the small heart and turned it around. She stared down at a teenage boy, a rebellious-looking youth with shaggy hair and a surly expression.

Kate drew in a gasp. She stared in amazement at a face she recognized, but one she hadn't expected to see. Even though the man's outer appearance had altered from the sullen teenager in the picture: his hair with sandy cast instead of dark — the bold eyes remained the same. Jake Pierson, now a curator at the local museum, had undergone a great change from the wild adolescent Kingsley had prohibited his niece from marrying years ago. This discovery, this connection, made all the information Kate had gathered about the case snap together.

'What are you doing in my room?'

Mary Ellen entered cautiously, placing on the dresser some object wrapped in a tan sweater. She was dressed in the same outfit she had worn when she had visited Pierson at the museum. Her chic clothing and carefully styled hair contrasted sharply with the unflattering glasses, that today she had not changed to contacts.

'You have no right snooping in my room.'

'I didn't know you were leaving today,' Kate said, laying the photograph on the bed beside the suitcase. As she did, her eyes lighted on the package wrapped in brown paper she had noticed earlier. This time she noted the shape of it, oblong, like a sheet of paper, the exact size of the frame downstairs that held the famous Tom Horn document.

'So you've come to say goodbye,' Mary Ellen said snappishly. 'How sweet. But as you can see, I'm busy packing. Jake will be here in a few minutes, and we're leaving together. For good.'

'I'm afraid you're going to have to stay a while longer,' Kate returned.

Mary Ellen gave an irritable wave of her hand as if trying to brush Kate's words aside. 'I have to be ready when he gets here.'

Kate stood poised over the suitcase. 'First I want to see what's in that package.'

'What are you searching for? You'll find nothing in there.'

'Then you won't mind if I take a look.' Quickly Kate snatched up the package, ripped the brown paper away, and revealed the framed document. 'This is the original invitation to Tom Horn's hanging. The one on the wall downstairs is a fake, a fake made by your boyfriend Jake Pierson.'

Mary Ellen looked stunned and lost, her large eyes draining of light and becoming singularly empty. 'Jake was always so smart,' she said in a quiet little voice. 'He loves everything that has to do with history, especially the legend of Tom Horn.' She added mournfully, 'That's what caused all the trouble for us years ago. Jake got drunk one night and broke into the house so he could steal it. But my uncle caught him and told him he was never to set foot on Rocking C property, and that he was never ever to see me again. If he so much as called me, my uncle was going to bring charges against him.'

'But he did return here.'

'He came back three years ago, so changed I would scarcely have known him. He had gone back to school, said he wanted to be able to offer me security so we could marry.' She drew herself up in a proud, but pathetic way. 'People around here think I don't have a life, but I do. Jake and I picked up right where we left off so many years ago.

'I wanted to marry him right away, but because of Uncle Charles' heart condition, Jake insisted that we wait. He said after all I'd put up with I deserved to inherit Uncle Charles' ranch.'

'The day he died, your uncle called you from Casper telling you he'd got married over the weekend.'

'He married her just to spite me,' Mary Ellen spat out. 'He'd found out Jake had come back to town and that I was seeing him again. After all the time and work I put in here, he planned to just disinherit me, to marry that floozy downstairs and cut me out with nothing.'

Kate waited, afraid that any prompting from her would stop the explanations that seemed to be pouring automatically from Mary Ellen's lips.

'I called Jake and told him what Charles had done and that I was going up to Casper to talk to him that evening. When Jake heard I'd been disinherited, he flew into a rage, said Uncle Charles had wrecked all of our plans again.'

Kate edged closer. She needed to be in a position to restrain Mary Ellen, if it came to that. Mary Ellen, aware of her plan, stepped back, maintaining the same distance between them.

'So Jake decided to steal for a second time what he had always had his eye on,' Kate said, 'that invitation to Tom Horn's hanging. Jake broke in to rob the Western collection while you were both gone. He didn't know that Mr Kingsley had come back to the ranch to talk to you before you had a chance to start for Casper. Kingsley heard Jake breaking in and came downstairs. Jake had worked at this ranch before, knew about the loaded weapon in the drawer and shot him with his own gun.'

'Jake didn't mean to kill him. He said

Charles attacked him. It was really self-defence.'

'So Jake put the stone he'd used to break the door window and placed it under your uncle's head in order to implicate Swen. Then before you had a chance to identify him, he fled.'

'Jake couldn't face me with what he'd done, but when I talked to him about the robbery,' Mary Ellen admitted, 'he confessed. I told him not to worry, I would help him cover up the crime.'

'You and Jake did all you could to place the blame on Swen. The first thing you did was destroy the folder concerning the pending lawsuit against Swen so he'd be the natural suspect.'

'Some lawsuit. All my uncle had were a few photos of Swen in his corral, trespassing.'

Kate noted the girl was becoming more and more agitated. She feared what would happen next, but she knew the only way to break her down was to keep her talking. Kate's voice rose, sounding to her own ears harsh and accusatory. 'You stole Swen's truck and rammed it into my squad car. You wanted me to think it was Swen trying to stop me from investigating him. You planted Jennie's earring and wrote her phone number on Swen's map in order to implicate her, too.'

'You're right. I found her earring in Charles' blue truck and came up with the idea. I hate Jennie more than I ever hated him. She's just a worthless gold-digger.'

'Did you know Jake was rustling cattle from both ranches?'

'Not until that night he confessed. He showed me his map, the places where he and Slim stole the cattle. But he promised that was all over, he wasn't going to steal anything ever again.'

'Then you were the one who wrote those x's on Swen's map along with Jennie's phone number. You found the gun Jake used, too, buried in the gazebo and hid it in a place where we couldn't find it.'

Stillness, sombre and heavy, hung between them. Mary Ellen took a step backwards. 'Don't look at me like that. Don't you see, we're not really to blame.'

'I'm sorry, Mary Ellen, but I'm going to have to take you in.'

Mary Ellen gave a little moan. She seemed to reel at Kate's words. She stumbled towards the dresser as if intending to use it to catch herself. Too late, Kate realized what she was doing. She freed the object she had brought with her into the room from its covering of sweater: a revolver, the Hawes .22, the gun that Pierson had used to murder her uncle. She aimed it directly at Kate's heart.

This swift action took Kate totally by surprise. She stood motionless, caught off guard, the way Charles Kingsley must have been right before Pierson had pulled the trigger.

In spite of the gun Mary Ellen looked like a frightened little girl. 'I'm leaving the Rocking C with Jake. No one can stop us.'

'You'll never get out of Belle County.'

Kate had no weapon. Only she, Mary Ellen, and Jennie were in the house, and she had left Jennie alone in the study, lost in her own world. If she screamed or made a sound, Jennie would start up the stairs and she would be in danger, too.

Muffled voices drifted up to them from downstairs. They both looked towards the door. 'She's in her room packing,' Jennie was saying. 'Just go on up.'

The creak of floorboards sounded as Jake Pierson's steps drew closer. Pierson appeared in the doorway, drawing to a halt when he saw the gun.

'What's going on here?'

Mary Ellen stammered, 'She knows everything, how you killed Uncle Charles and how I helped you cover up.'

Pierson's expression changed, merging in Kate's mind with the image of the boy in the photograph. Yet the sullenness had been replaced by a poisonous wrath.

Kate should have made the connection between Pierson and Slim Barton the day she had seen them together at the Lazy Z. 'You're willing to let Slim Barton take the fall for the cattle rustling.'

'It's all in his name. There's no proof to tie it to me. He knew what he was up against when I hired him.'

'Who shot me? You or Slim Barton?'

'Slim's the one who shot you. Then when you and Garrison went back to look for evidence, he was following. He saw you pick up the bullets, but I'm the one who got the proof you found back. I couldn't let Slim get caught and ruin our operation.'

So Jake Pierson had been the man in the ski mask who had waylaid her on the way to the sheriff's office. He had used Hal Barkley's car, which Slim had spotted the day she had run into him out at Barkley's place.

From the corner of her eye Kate saw Mary Ellen, her hand on the gun.

'I did it all for Mary Ellen.'

'You tried to steal Kingsley's Western collection and when you failed, you still wouldn't give up. You made that forgery of the invitation to Tom Horn's hanging and talked Mary Ellen into switching it for you. You were just using her because you wanted everything Kingsley had.'

'But all I really wanted was Mary Ellen.'

'That's not true,' Kate said. 'Money always came first with you, not Mary Ellen.'

Kate knew after the words left her lips she should never have spoken them. Pierson's cold eyes narrowed with hatred. Kate could do nothing but make a final plea to Mary Ellen, try to make her understand his treachery. 'For all your declarations of love, you have never cared about anyone but yourself and the Kingsley fortune. You even kept on rustling Kingsley's cattle after you had killed him.'

'But you promised me you had quit.' The gun lowered in Mary Ellen's hand, then lifted to Kate again.

Kate, seeing an advantage, pressed on, 'That greed is what ruined you. The x's Mary Ellen marked on Swen's map to mislead us, instead led us directly to the rustling sites.'

Pierson glared at Mary Ellen. 'After all I did for you, you go and mess it up. Now we don't have a penny.'

'We still have each other, Jake. And we

have that Tom Horn relic, which will give us enough money to make a new start. Let's tie her up and get out of here. Now!'

His eyes shifted back to Kate. 'We can't leave any witnesses.' He added, his voice deadly quiet, 'Give me the gun, Mary Ellen.'

Mary Ellen stared at him, realization pouring over her, as if she had just been struck by the fact that her uncle had been right about Jake Pierson all along.

Kate waited immobile, her breath catching in her throat.

Mary Ellen's hand shook as the revolver wavered between them. She took several uncertain steps toward Pierson, then with a sob turned and pressed the gun into Kate's hands.

'We never would have caught Pierson, Kate, if you hadn't noticed that forgery,' Ben said, munching happily on a doughnut. He had been released from the hospital with orders for a strict diet that Kate was pretty certain didn't include chocolate-tops.

Ben finished his pastry, took a sip of coffee and said, 'Jake Pierson masterminded all these crimes. He used Mary Ellen and Slim for his own purposes.'

'That boy was always a bad egg,' Lem responded. 'Even though he had left that girl alone for years, once he heard about Charles' ill health he decided to step right in and court Mary Ellen again. He had pretended to go straight, got that job at the museum. He didn't care whether Charles recognized him or not.'

'And that was his first mistake,' Kate said. 'The minute Kingsley found out Pierson was seeing his niece again, he changed his will. He couldn't stand by and let his empire fall into the hands of a man like that.

'The trouble started years ago when Pierson tried to get his hands on that invitation to Tom Horn's hanging. When Kingsley caught him red-handed, it was a blow to his pride. He never got over wanting that bit of paper, which in his mind was linked to the loss of his girlfriend and his chance of ever becoming a cattle baron like Kingsley.

'He intended to steal the invitation even after he had shot Kingsley, but Mary Ellen's being home that night prevented it. Still he couldn't let it go. When he found out Jennie was never going to sell the collection, the idea occurred to him to make a forgery. He insisted Mary Ellen make the switch and that's what caused him to get caught.'

'How did you know that Tom Horn invitation was a forgery, Prep?' Jeff asked with a tinge of admiration.

'It was too perfect. The forgery had a crease and an inkblot that wasn't on the original. He used authentic paper he got from the museum's storage room and a special type of ink formula used in the late 1880s and early 1900s. The documents specialist we called in ran ultraviolet and infrared light examinations, so when the case comes to trial, we'll have definite proof of what he did.'

'Jake Pierson was too smart for his own good.' Ben laughed. 'That's what trips up most criminals.'

'How did you make the link between this crime and Mary Ellen's old boyfriend?' Jeff asked.

'I knew the criminal had to have an in-depth knowledge of Wyoming history; more-over a familiarity with the layout of both ranches and the long-established rivalry of Swen and Kingsley. Because he had worked for Kingsley once, Mary Ellen's old boy-friend sprang to mind. I got to figuring he must have returned, but I suspected he was Slim Barton, not Jake Pierson.'

Kate continued, 'Pierson made a threaten-ing phone call to me the night of the cook-off. He heard me asking questions about Mary Ellen's old boyfriend and knew if I kept looking I'd soon be able to identify him.'

'I can't help but feel sorry for Mary Ellen,' Lem said. 'Probably when she was real young, Pierson did all he could to poison her mind against her uncle. Of course she resented Kingsley for keeping them apart all these years. What do you suppose will happen to her now?'

'She wasn't involved in the cattle rustling and she had no part in the Kingsley shooting,' Ben said. 'But she will be charged with aiding and abetting a criminal.'

'She saved my life,' Kate spoke up. 'My testimony might help her.'

Jeff rose, saying, 'It's time we got back to work, Lem.' At the door, he turned to Kate. 'Prep,' he said with a slow smile, 'I'm going to admit it. From the first, you were right and I was wrong.'

'Would you write that down and have it notarized?'

'Not likely,' Jeff said with a chuckle.

'No wonder you believed Swen was guilty. Pierson did everything possible to make him the fall guy, even to placing that stone under Kingsley's head. To me that was Pierson's big mistake. He should have made it look like an ordinary robbery instead of a crime of vengeance.'

Lem followed Jeff out of Ben's office. Kate started to leave, too, but was stopped by Ben's words. 'Not so fast.'

Jeff had told Kate her future with the department depended entirely on Ben Addison. Dread filled her. She had made big mistakes whilst working this case, and from the sheriff's tone she was going to pay for them now. He would either dismiss her or at the very least hit her with a long suspension. Disobeying orders was something Ben would never let slide.

Kate paused, her hand on the doorknob. For a moment she felt tearful. It would be hard to leave the job she loved so much, to bid farewell to Rock Creek, Wyoming.

Steeling herself, she turned to face him. 'So what happens now?'

'Well, let's see.' Ben reminded her of Jeff and the way he began recounting her misdeeds. 'You disobeyed orders, you stubbornly pursued the case long after you should have stopped.' He gave her a long look. 'In other words, you did exactly what I would have done.'

She gazed at him, unable to believe his words. 'I'm sorry for all the mistakes,' she said sincerely.

'We're all human.' Ben studied the carton of doughnuts before him, then remembering the doctor's orders, with all the will-power he could muster, pushed them away. 'You do the best you can. That's all people can ask of you.'

'Then you're not firing me?'

'For what? For making the Belle County sheriff's department look good?' He leaned forward slightly, his heavy weight causing a protesting squeak. 'Deputy Jepp,' he said, 'we never could have solved the Kingsley murder case without you.' He reached into the drawer beside him and slid her gun and badge across the desk, then using the exact words Kate had spoken to him in the hospital, he reminded her, 'Not everyone gets a second chance.'

G
29.95

MAR - - 2009